NUGGETS FROM COORG HISTORY

Other books by the author:

Victoria Gowramma: The Lost Princess of Coorg
Tongue of the Slip: Looking Back on Life with Humour

NUGGETS FROM COORG HISTORY

REVISED AND UPDATED EDITION

C.P. BELLIAPPA

Published by
Rupa Publications India Pvt. Ltd 2008, 2015
7/16, Ansari Road, Daryaganj
New Delhi 110002

Sales centres:
Bengaluru Chennai
Hyderabad Jaipur Kathmandu
Kolkata Mumbai Prayagraj

Copyright © C.P. Belliappa 2008, 2015

The views and opinions expressed in this book are the author's own and the facts are as reported by him which have been verified to the extent possible, and the publishers are not in any way liable for the same.

All rights reserved.
No part of this publication may be reproduced, transmitted, or stored in a retrieval system, in any form or by any means, electronic, mechanical, photocopying, recording or otherwise, without the prior permission of the publisher.

P-ISBN: 978-81-291-1302-3
E-ISBN: 978-81-291-2667-2

Eleventh impression 2024

15 14 13 12 11

The moral right of the author has been asserted.

Printed in India

This book is sold subject to the condition that it shall not, by way of trade or otherwise, be lent, resold, hired out, or otherwise circulated, without the publisher's prior consent, in any form of binding or cover other than that in which it is published.

When the world was without a king
and dispersed in fear in all directions,
The Lord created a king
for the protection of all.

...Even an infant king must not be despised,
as though a mere mortal,
For he is a great god
in human form.

—Manu

CONTENTS

Preface ix

Dawn of the Haleri Dynasty 1
Acchu Nayaka of Anchigeri 8
Story of Alamanda Doddavva 15
Utha Nayaka 22
Siribai Veerappa Raja 28
Hyder Ali and Tipu Sultan in Coorg 35
A Kingdom Nearly Lost 41
Veerarajendra's Escapades and a Brief History of Virajpet 49
A Kingdom Regained 56
Last Will and Testament of Veerarajendra 64
Lingarajendra the Lucky 72
Story of Thathanda Subbayya 80
The Omkareshwara Temple 89
Haleri Rajas and the British 95
Dewan Kunta Basava's Role in the Fall of Haleri Dynasty 99
Chikka Veerarajendra's Exile 109

Kongettira Rani Kaverammaji	117
The British in Coorg	126
Christianity in Coorg	134
Maharaja Duleep Singh and Princess Victoria Gowramma	140
Freedom Movement in Coorg	150
Genesis of Merger of Coorg with Karnataka	157
Glossary	163
References	166
Acknowledgements	167

PREFACE

Compared with the gigantic extent of the Indian Peninsula, Coorg is but of a baby's size however large it may appear to its inhabitants.

—Rev. G. Richter

Rev. G. Richter was one of the first Englishmen to compile a comprehensive history of this tiny province of Coorg (Kodagu) in his *Gazetteer of Coorg* published in 1870. He drew a great deal of his material from previous writings on Coorg, especially those by Lieutenant Connor of Royal Engineers, and Rev. Hermann Moegling, the German Protestant evangelist's *Coorg Memoirs* published in 1855. Early history of the Haleri dynasty was recorded in *Rajendraname*, which was commissioned by Dodda Veerarajendra in 1808. General Robert Abercrombie, a contemporary and friend of Dodda Veerarajendra, later translated *Rajendraname* to English.

The rajas of the Haleri dynasty, who ruled Coorg from around 1600 till 1834, were alien to Coorg and the local culture. Haleri rajas were Lingayats. The prominent community of Coorg comprised of the Coorgs (Kodavas), who were basically ancestor and nature worshippers. Kodavas soon adopted many aspects of Hinduism and were deeply influenced by the Brahmins, and are now categorized as Hindus. Over the years a strong bond was forged between the Lingayat rajas and the

Kodavas, which lasted for more than two centuries. In spite of instances of highhandedness during the reign of the last three rajas, Kodavas remained loyal. This may be attributed to the belief that rajas were ordained to rule by divine right as propounded by Manu. Finally, it was part folly of the last raja—Chikka Veerarajendra—and part intrigues of the British East India Company that ultimately brought an end to the dynasty in 1834.

Coorg first attracted the attention of the British in their quest to overthrow Tipu Sultan of Mysore. Tipu Sultan and his father Hyder Ali were both disliked by the Haleri rajas as well as the Kodavas. As a result, Coorg became a willing ally of the British in fighting the 'Tiger of Mysore'. The geographic location of Coorg was of great strategic value to both Tipu as well as the British. The tactical and logistical help provided by Dodda Veerarajendra to the British proved to be of vital importance in the defeat of Tipu Sultan in 1799.

The British settlers who came to Coorg after its annexation in 1834 were clearly smitten by this land. Most of them, experienced in coffee cultivation, shifted from Sri Lanka primarily with a view to exploit the potential of growing coffee here. Coorg was a thickly forested area full of wild beasts. It was adventure coupled with the prospect of owning a plantation that attracted the British to venture into this inhospitable area. They got on well with the local population who too later followed the British in opening coffee estates. The settlers found the weather and the hilly landscape similar to that in some parts of Britain and nostalgically referred to Coorg as the 'Scotland of India'.

The only Indian who carried out extensive research on

Coorg history was D.N. Krishnayya, who was a teacher in the government school in Mercara. His book, written in Kannada, titled *Kodagina Ithihasa* (History of Coorg) is a treasure trove of interesting anecdotes and details collected from earlier accounts, and through his interactions with some of the elders in Coorg families during the 1930s. I have gathered a great deal of information on Coorg history from Krishnayya's book, which was first published in 1974. I pay my tribute to Krishnayya for recording some important facts about the history of this region, which would have otherwise been lost with the passage of time.

In this book, I have gleaned interesting episodes pertaining to Coorg history and have dramatized the stories to some extent in order to make them interesting to the reader. In this, I have followed the dictum of Aristotle who once famously said:

> 'The dramatized representation of history is a more scientific and serious pursuit than the exact writing of history.'

All the events and dates, however, are factual.

I have a personal connection with the history of Coorg. My great-great-great-grandfather, Dewan Chepudira Ponnappa, served the last three rajas of Coorg. The East India Company retained him as a dewan after the annexation of Coorg. His sons and grandsons held important positions under the British rule. However, his great-great-grandson C.M. Poonacha (my father) was one of the leading figures from Coorg in the freedom movement, and was the chief minister of Coorg State from 1952 to 1956.

The history of Coorg could at best be a footnote in the hoary past of India. It is, however, the collective chronicle of what happened in every nook and corner of this complex land that makes the history of India fascinating. There is a common historic bond that encompasses India that is 'Bharat'.

In this updated and revised edition, I have added two more chapters—'Haleri Rajas and the British', and 'Freedom Movement in Coorg'. The original text has also been enhanced with additional details. Some more images have been added as well. With this updating, the readers will get a more complete narrative of the history of Coorg (Kodagu).

Note: In this book, I have used interchangeable names: Kodagu and Coorg, Kodavas and Coorgs, Madikeri and Mercara.

HALERI DYNASTY

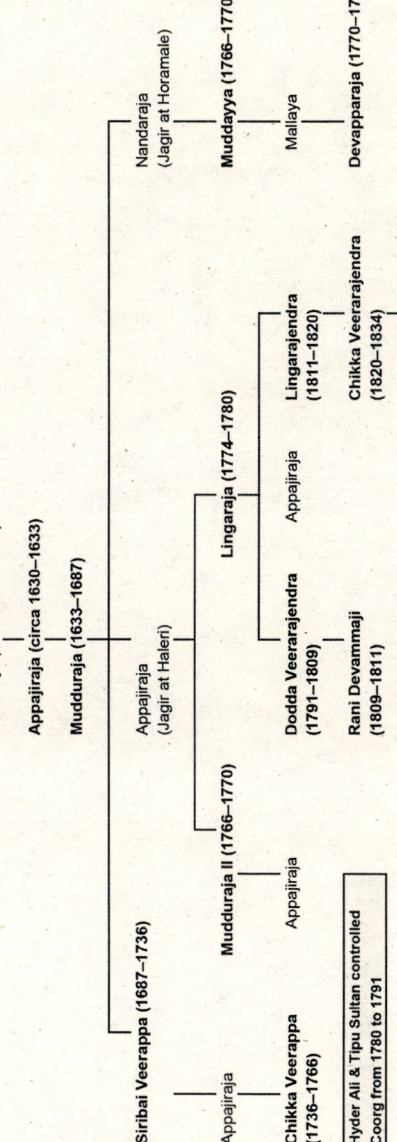

Note: Many of the names of the members of the Haleri dynasty are repeated in every generation. Names of female members too are repeated quite often.

DAWN OF THE HALERI DYNASTY

The six-year-old Veeraraja tugged at his mother's sari and queried, 'Mother, when am I going to be crowned a nayaka?' He was sitting next to his parents at the investiture of his uncle Sadashiva, who as heir-apparent had succeeded Chowdappa Nayaka, the founder of the Ikkeri dynasty. Veeraraja's mother patted him and whispered, 'When you have a kingdom of your own my son.'

The young boy was inspired by the imperious and commanding personality of his uncle. He dreamed of emulating Sadashiva Nayaka who was an ambitious ruler. He started his reign from their capital at Ikkeri, a small village near Shimoga. One of the first tasks he undertook after ascending the throne was to improve the fortification of the capital. The Ikkeri rulers were under the tutelage of the powerful Vijayanagar Empire. With their support and patronage, Sadashiva Nayaka extended his influence up to Mangalore in the south.

As the years rolled by, young Veeraraja got frustrated with his barren jagir in the dusty village of Arakalagod in Hassan. He grew more and more envious of his uncle, and was determined to better his lot. He did not want to remain just a minor princeling involved in farming. His mother's words kept ringing in his ears and, early in life, he set his goal to be a ruler, a king of his own dominion and a founder of a dynasty. Veeraraja firmly believed that he was destined to be a ruler. There was, however, no scope for him to challenge or replace the powerful Sadashiva Nayaka or his successors who were all well-entrenched in their territories.

By the time the Vijayanagar Empire fell to the onslaught of the Deccan Sultanate in 1565 AD, Sadashiva Nayaka's descendant, Venkatappa Nayaka, was in power. With the disintegration of the Empire, most of the smaller kingdoms were conquered by their dominant neighbours. Taking full advantage of the opportunity, Venkatappa Nayaka added many of the splintered territories to his realm, extending his influence now from Honnavar in North Kanara to Chandragiri in South Kanara.

Veeraraja by then had matured into a robust young man with an imposing personality. He was an active member of the Ikkeri army of Venkatappa Nayaka and had taken part in several military expeditions and gained valuable experience in warfare. Veeraraja was a restless soul and spent a great deal of his spare time secretly exploring the regions in the neighbourhood with a small band of his supporters. He diligently sought a territory where he could exploit the weakness of the local rulers to his advantage. In his quest for a kingdom, the over-ambitious Veeraraja had developed a ruthless streak.

In around 1600 AD, Veeraraja's peregrinations brought him close to the northern border of the mountainous land of Kodagu, perched on the Western Ghats. This was the period when great events were taking place in the rest of the world—the Mughal ruler Shahenshah Akbar controlled most of northern India, and Queen Elizabeth-I sat on the throne of England. The actions of these powerful rulers and their legacy had repercussions in India centuries after their demise. It was in 1599 that Queen Elizabeth-I awarded the royal charter to the fledgling East India

Company to trade in India. Veeraraja had heard of the fertile land of Kodagu, which was covered with dense forests. The prominent inhabitants of this land were the battle-hardened Kodavas. Kodagu was home to a variety of wild flora and fauna, poisonous snakes, deadly insects and blood-sucking leeches. The monsoon was torrential and lasted for well over six months in a year. One had to be extremely brave to live here, and not many outsiders ventured into this inhospitable terrain. Veeraraja nonetheless envisioned great potential in the area.

Veeraraja's spies, who infiltrated into Kodagu, brought him news of intense infighting amongst the fractious Kodava warlords who called themselves nayakas. The fall of the Vijayanagar Empire had exposed the rifts between these chieftains who were at war with one another to consolidate their hold on their dominions. The more ambitious among them invaded their neighbours marking a period of relentless hostilities. Each nayaka had demarcated his land by digging deep defensive trenches known as kadangas. These kadangas are still in evidence at several parts of Kodagu, reflecting the deep fissures which divided the Kodava nayakas.

Veeraraja gauged that the time was ripe to try his luck in Kodagu. He made his first appearance in the hamlets of the northern parts of Kodagu, disguised in the garb of a priest popularly known as jangama. He gradually moved southwards and earned the patronage of the local nayaka. Veeraraja quietly built a few innocuous huts and settled in Haleri village along with a few of his followers. Dressed as a poor jangama, he projected a humble demeanour. One day, he approached the nayaka with folded hands and requested: 'O powerful nayaka, kindly permit me to build a temple and a religious mutt in your territory. Lord Shiva's blessings will be on you and your family.' Perceiving no threat the naive nayaka agreed.

In the prevailing situation of political uncertainty, the superstitious nayakas of Kodagu were gradually coming under the influence of priests, soothsayers, exorcists and astrologers. For centuries, Kodavas had worshipped their ancestors. They revered as well as feared nature and paid obeisance to the river goddess Kavery and the forest god Ayyappa. Besides the nayakas, the common Kodavas too got attracted to Hindu deities introduced by the priests and Brahmins from the neighbouring areas. They, however, continued worshipping their ancestors, guru karana, and nature. Every village had a sacred grove known as Devarakadu, where the forest deities were believed to be residing. These swathes of forests were maintained in their pristine conditions and no cultivation or hunting was permitted. It was only since the twentieth century that most of these sacred groves were encroached upon.

Veeraraja, being a Lingayat, was well-versed in performing poojas, religious ceremonies and astrological rituals. He was equally adept at casting spells and in conducting séances. He was a medicine man as well, and knew preparations of Ayurvedic potions. Equipped with these skills, he soon gained popularity, and his imposing persona attracted more followers. His reputation spread in the neighbouring areas, and some of the nayakas invited him for advice and treatment of ailments. The farmers who benefited from his medicines and astrological predictions started voluntarily contributing a small part of their leftover dusty paddy crop (referred to as 'dhulli-batha') for use at his religious mutt.

Within a few years, Veeraraja gained sufficient support and

loyalty to establish a parallel centre of power in Haleri. He deftly overthrew the local nayaka with the connivance of the hopelessly divided Kodavas who helped Veeraraja succeed in his cunning schemes. Once in control, he imposed his authority on the people of Haleri. With a firm foothold in Haleri, he now demanded substantially more paddy (of the superior quality) and other farm produce to be supplied to his mutt. His granary swelled with food grains. To protect his assets, he built a mud-walled fortification around the mutt. With his newfound wealth, he employed guards to provide security to his family and followers. Soon, he had a formidable body of well-trained Kodava men who could intimidate any adversary. Quite a few of the nayakas in the neighbouring areas came under his influence and started paying tribute to Veeraraja in return for his protection. His growing power also made him a mediator in feuds between the nayakas. Very often, he himself instigated fights between the gullible warlords. Haleri, a sleepy village known for producing large quantities of milk, now became the hub of Veeraraja's growing authority. Subsequently, his connection to the Ikkeri dynasty was revealed to the people. With his unquestioned power and revelation of royal lineage, people started referring to him as the raja of Haleri. A few years later, he subdued some of the prominent nayakas in the northern parts of Kodagu and soon his army became one of the strongest in the area.

The only force to reckon with, that continued to pose a threat to Veeraraja's ambitions, was the powerful Kodava nayaka named Karenembau who ruled Bhagamandala and Tala-Kavery—the source of river Kavery. For Veeraraja to achieve his dream of establishing his own kingdom and gaining undisputed control of the region, Karenembau had to be defeated. Though well past his prime, Veeraraja patiently planned his move and mustered sufficient armed men to cross swords with Karenembau. Owing to infighting amongst the Kodavas, Karenembau failed in his attempts at spearheading a combined army of Kodava nayakas to check the advances of the foreigner Veeraraja. After protracted battle, Veeraraja gained an upper-hand and subsequently massacred Karenembau and his forces. This was a significant victory for Veeraraja. He mercilessly eliminated most of the nayakas who dared resist his authority. Those who surrendered, accepted him as their lord and master, paying heavy tribute. With his protectorate having extended to most of the land, Veeraraja gained sufficient self-confidence to declare himself the raja of Kodagu. He shed his sackcloth-and-ashes to don the more martial kupiya-chele worn by the local Kodavas. Subsequently, he designated his son Appajiraja as his heir-apparent. This was the beginning of the Haleri dynasty of Lingayat rulers in Kodagu. Within two decades of his stepping into Kodagu, Veeraraja had fulfilled his dream of establishing his own kingdom and dynasty.

After the eventful reign of Veeraraja, his son Appajiraja ascended the throne of Kodagu. During his brief rule, Appajiraja maintained the dominance established by his father, and was succeeded by his able son Mudduraja in 1633.

Mudduraja reigned for the longest period, that is fifty-four years. During this period, he further consolidated the Haleri dynasty's position and hold on Kodagu. In a wise move, he shifted the capital from the remote Haleri to the more strategically located Madikeri in 1681. He chose the location of the fort at Madikeri while on a hunting trip in the region;

when he was astonished to see a hare chase one of his hunting dogs! Mudduraja inferred that the land was veera-boomi and hence ideal for the construction of a fort. Mudduraja interacted closely with his people and was a popular ruler. The Kodavas had grown weary of constant conflicts between the nayakas. They welcomed peace and stability ushered in by Mudduraja and his predecessors. Mudduraja's reign endeared the citizens to the regime of Haleri kings. Some of the nayakas still controlled parts of southern Kodagu even though they paid fealty to Mudduraja. Mudduraja's son Siribai Veerappa vanquished the remaining nayakas, and by mid-eighteenth century brought all of Kodagu and some of the territories in Sullya in South Kanara under the absolute rule of the Haleri dynasty.

ACCHU NAYAKA OF ANCHIGERI

It was around end August circa 1650, and the heavy monsoon rains were gradually receding from the Western Ghats. Kattemane Chittiappa Nayaka surveyed his territory, Anchigeri, from the ramparts of his mud fort. The paddy fields had been cultivated meticulously that year; the important activity of transplanting had been completed well in time, soon after the onset of the monsoon in June. His people were grateful to him for mobilising all the available resources required for paddy cultivation. Chittiappa on his part was pleased at the sight of the terraced fields swaying with paddy, which had started to take on the healthy dark green hue promising a good harvest. The paddy crop would be ready for harvesting only in December, and till then the villagers did not have much to do. The women folk would attend to the occasional weeding required on the fields. Chittiappa and his men looked forward to long hunting trips into the forest, and the lazy evenings eating bush-meat and drinking the local brew, toddy. More importantly, there were no impending threats from any of the nayakas in the neighbourhood and peace reigned supreme. In the meantime, Chittiappa Nayaka had strengthened the fortification around the village and had deepened the kadangas. His father and grandfather had to pay tribute to the Vijayanagar Empire but after the Empire collapsed, the nayakas had become independent, and all the income of their dominion remained with them. Chittiappa invested the surplus funds in strengthening his army with better training and improved weaponry.

The Kailpodu festival, which marked the end of monsoon and the beginning of the hunting season, was celebrated with great fervour that September. Chittiappa and his men carried out the ritual cleaning and oiling of all their weapons. Sandalwood paste was smeared on the weapons which were then decorated with flowers. The weapons were considered to be a symbol of their ancestors. They invoked the blessings of their guru karanas, the ancestors, for a bountiful harvest and success in hunting. The celebration was followed by a feast with plenty of toddy flowing late into the night.

This idyllic condition, however, did not last long. The day after Kailpodu, Chittiappa Nayaka received news from his spies that their neighbour and rival, Mukkatira Nayaka of Mathur village, had made a foray into the forest, which separated their territories, to hunt a marauding tiger. The beast had been lifting cattle and other livestock but when it started attacking people, the villagers from Mathur sought their nayaka's help. Mukkatira Nayaka's subjects promised their chief a grand 'nari-mangala' or a wedding celebration with the slain tiger, if he got rid of the prowling beast. However, both the nayakas had laid their claim on the patch of forest which had long been a bone of contention between the two. This news of hunting in the disputed area infuriated Chittiappa and he ordered his men to immediately get ready for the tiger hunt. He wanted to be the one to bag the trophy as well as the glory.

Chittiappa and his men entered the forest with their hunting dogs amidst reverberating sounds of drum-beating. It was hot and humid in the forest and the undergrowth had grown thick during the monsoon. An advance team of Chittiappa's men had to clear the jungle before the hunting party could move ahead. Their progress was slowed down further as they had to contend with mosquitoes and leeches at every step. Meanwhile, Mukkatira Nayaka and his team had already started chasing the tiger from the opposite direction. The terrified tiger ran towards Anchigeri village. In its effort to get away from the pursuing hunters, the animal came almost face to face with Chittiappa Nayaka and his group of shikaris. Seizing the moment, Chittiappa felled the tiger with a single shot, as it crouched to pounce on him.

Anchigeri villagers were ecstatic. They triumphantly carried the slain beast to their village, singing praises of their leader Chittiappa Nayaka. The following day the 'nari-mangala' was celebrated in great style in Anchigeri village. Mukkatira Nayaka fumed at his adversary for having 'stolen the thunder' from him. This entire episode tarnished the image of Mukkatira Nayaka not only in the neighbouring domains but also amongst his own people. He felt slighted, and with revenge in mind he approached another neighbouring nayaka, Machangala Nayaka, who too was envious of Chittiappa Nayaka's growing fame and popularity. Together they hatched a plot to attack and wipe out Chittiappa Nayaka and his family. Machangala Nayaka insisted that their attack should be a stealthy one under the cover of darkness. Mukkatira Nayaka was initially not in favour of this cowardly scheme. However, he was persuaded and was convinced by Machangala Nayaka that their powerful adversary could be eliminated only by devious means.

The following night two hundred armed men were led by Mukkatira Nayaka and Machangala Nayaka to Anchigeri village.

The mission was kept a secret until the last moment lest their adversary get wind of the attack. The 'nari-mangala' celebration had exhausted Chittiappa and his people. Plenty of toddy had been consumed, and the men were in a stupor. The attackers quietly surrounded Chittiappa Nayaka's battlement. The sentries outside the walls were fast asleep and were disposed of easily. Some of the dogs barked, but the people inside Chittiappa's household did not respond. After eliminating the guards, the soldiers entered the fort and encircled the house. They then set fire to the structure by shooting flaming arrows on the thatched roof. The dwelling, which was built of bamboo, wood and straw, was soon engulfed in roaring flames. Chittiappa Nayaka and his people were rudely awakened and they immediately started defending themselves. Chittiappa Nayaka rushed to the front of the house and fought gallantly cutting down several of his foes. However, being hopelessly outnumbered, it turned out to be a losing battle for Chittiappa and his family. Many perished in the blaze, and Chittiappa himself died while fighting.

In this commotion, a young maidservant named Ayyavva managed to bundle the two-year-old son of Chittiappa and escape from the inferno. On being confronted by the soldiers, Ayyavva somehow convinced them that the child was her own, and pleaded that they be spared. The rival nayakas' soldiers let her go but warned her, 'Don't ever set foot in Anchigeri village again.'

Overnight, Ayyavva carried the infant through Mathur village and found shelter in the farm of Mookachanda family of Amma Kodavas. The Mookachanda family kept them in their house for a few days, but advised her to move away lest they themselves invite the nayakas' wrath. With their help, Ayyavva and the child found their way to next-door Periapatna, ruled at the time by the descendants of Chengalvas. Ayyavva found work as a maid in a rich merchant's house and raised the son of Chittiappa Nayaka, whom she affectionately called 'Acchu'.

Acchu grew well and by the time he was about seven years old, he was a good-looking young lad. The ruler at Periapatna at that time was Nanjunda Urs. During the Ugadhi festival, it was the practice of the raja and his consorts to go on a procession. All the citizenry came on to the main street to see the king and his family dressed in their royal regalia riding elephants, horses and some being carried in palanquins. Ayyavva brought Acchu to witness this grand event. As Nanjunda Urs passed by, he noticed the bright-faced Acchu and was sure that the boy was of noble birth. He was curious to know who the youngster was. He sent his men to bring Acchu to his palace that evening.

A nervous Ayyavva took the boy to the palace and was immediately taken to the raja. Nanjunda Urs put her at ease. He asked her her name and that of the boy's. She hesitatingly told the raja that Acchu was her son. 'You can tell me the truth, and no harm will come to you or the boy,' said Nanjuda Urs with an understanding smile. After a moment's hesitation she narrated the story of Acchu's father Chittiappa Nayaka and the tragic destruction of his family. Nanjunda Urs had sons of Acchu's age. He offered to keep Acchu in his palace as a companion to his children. Ayyavva too was given a job in the palace. Acchu demonstrated his intelligence and skills at learning. Along with the princes, he too got trained in statecraft and in the art of handling a variety of weapons. He was a quick learner and a good horseman as well. By the time he turned twenty, he was an able warrior and proved to be an asset to the raja. He was loyal, trustworthy, and close to the royal household.

Over the years, Acchu learnt all about his father and family in detail from Ayyavva, his foster mother. He yearned to go back to his homeland. One day he requested Nanjunda Urs, 'Please give me an army of five hundred men to take back my father's realm and avenge the brutal killings of my family by the Mukkatira and Machangala nayakas.' Nanjunda Urs obliged him with a posse of soldiers. Consequently, Acchu set forth on his mission to reconquer his lost realm.

On hearing that Chittiappa Nayaka's son was marching towards Anchigeri with a strong army, both the Mukkatira Nayaka and Machangala Nayaka developed cold feet. They were quite old by then and realized that they would be no match against Acchu and his well-armed men. Keeping their own safety in mind, they fled south to Wynad to escape the fury of Chittiappa's son. The people of Anchigeri welcomed Acchu and accepted him as their new nayaka. In addition to his father's domain, he also took control of the territories ruled by the Mukkatira and Machangala nayakas.

In the years that followed, Acchu Nayaka ruled his territories wisely and enhanced the standard of living of his people. He built a fort and a palace in Chikkamudoor village, with a deep moat around it to protect the fort. He erected a kaimada or a mantap near the fort in honour of his mentor and installed in it a statue of Nanjunda Urs. A reservoir established in front of the kaimada and the kaimada itself are still in existence. (There is still evidence of the blaze that destroyed Chittiappa Nayaka's fortress more than three centuries ago. Burnt paddy can still be found if the earth is dug in the place where the granary once stood.)

Kaimada built by Acchu Nayaka (circa 1700)

At the time of Acchu Nayaka's reign in Kiggatnad, the Haleri king Mudduraja ruled from Haleri and was slowly spreading his control over Kodagu. Acchu Nayaka was unhappy with the growing power of the Haleri rajas. He was troubled at the rapid transformation of the Kodavas—their form of worship and way of life. The increasing influence of Brahmins and priests amongst the people had also started to bother him. However, he still maintained cordial relationships with Mudduraja, and for his protection, he had to pay tribute to the Haleri raja.

STORY OF ALAMANDA DODDAVVA

Alamanda family was a prominent clan in Kodagu. By around 1630, Ayyappa was the only surviving male member of his okka. His brothers and cousins had fallen victims to malaria while still in their youth. As the sole male member of his patrilineal family, Ayyappa inherited a large property owned by the clan in Armeri village in Beppunad, in southern part of Kodagu.

Ayyappa was an enterprising and energetic farmer. He extended his landholding and started growing other crops besides paddy. He was one of the earliest cultivators in Kodagu of the highly valued cardamom. In addition, Ayyappa started a wholesale business of supplying paddy to Kannur in Kerala from where he procured salt and other provisions for distribution in Armeri and the nearby villages.

Although his business and farming flourished, Ayyappa was not a happy man since even after six years of marriage he and his wife remained childless. They longed for a family, and Ayyappa was anxious for a son to inherit his fortune and also continue the lineage of the nearly extinct Alamanda clan. Some of the villagers suggested that Ayyappa take another wife. However, he dismissed the idea putting his faith in Alamanda guru karanas or ancestors—to bless them with a progeny. With this in view, the couple visited several temples and consulted astrologers from Kerala and South Kanara. Ayyappa and his wife were given various potions by the tantrics, which they were assured, would enhance fertility. Their morale was boosted when they were comforted by all whom they consulted, that the family bloodline would continue.

A couple of years later, a humble old soothsayer from the neighbouring village predicted, 'A daughter will soon be born, and she will be better than half a dozen sons.' Ayyappa and his wife were not too excited with this forecast. It was the birth of a male heir that they had prayed for. One fine morning, Ayyappa's wife informed him that she was pregnant with his child. Ayyappa was ecstatic. The news soon spread in the village, and it became a favourite topic of discussion. Wagers were taken if the prediction of the soothsayer would come true or not. Ayyappa and his wife hoped that the fortune-teller would be wrong, and that they would be blessed with a son.

On Kavery Sankaramana day, Ayyappa's wife gave birth to a chubby child, at about the same time when the holy water emerged from the pond at Tala-Kavery. For Kodavas, this is considered an auspicious time for the birth of a child. However, the soothsayer was right—it was a beautiful baby girl. Though disappointed, Ayyappa and his wife welcomed the arrival of their daughter as a gift from goddess Kavery. They named the baby Kaveramma, after the river goddess.

Kaveramma was an unusual baby. She surprised her parents by starting to walk, talk and learn things faster than any other child of her age. Even as a toddler, her temperament was determined and assertive, and she invariably had her way. Soon Kaveramma proved to be such a delightful young girl that she endeared herself to all the people in the village.

By the time Kaveramma was ten years old, she had grown

taller and stronger than the boys her age, outdoing them in most of the games and outdoor activities.

When Kaveramma was around twelve years old her father asked her, 'What would you like from Kannur?' She promptly replied, 'All I want is to come with you to Kannur.' After much discussion between the parents, it was finally decided that Ayyappa would take her along to Kannur on his business trip. The journey by bullock-cart on the winding mountainous roads was an arduous task, but Kaveramma enjoyed every moment of the outing and was most inquisitive about the new places they passed by. At Kannur, she was overawed by the sight of the sea for the first time. The young girl quickly grasped the intricacies of business and in time started helping her father in various business transactions. Ayyappa was immensely pleased with his only child's abilities. He now realized that his daughter was indeed as good as a son.

By the time she turned fifteen, Kaveramma grew to be an attractive and statuesque young woman. She assisted her father in all the activities, be it on the paddy field or in their business. She could ride a bullock-cart, plough the fields and keep accounts of the business dealings. The workers in the Alamanda property admiringly referred to her as Doddavva, or the great lady. As years rolled by, she came to be popularly known as Doddavva.

Offers for Doddavva's hand in marriage started pouring in from nearby villages and as far away in Kodagu. As an heir to the Alamanda family fortune, she was a highly eligible young woman. However, Ayyappa, now quite old, wanted his own family line, Alamanda, to continue. The only way this could be achieved was by making the young man who married Doddavva to forego his stake in his own clan and take on the family name of Alamanda. This practice, known as 'okka-parije', was permitted amongst Kodavas in rare cases such as Doddavva's where the patriarchal family would otherwise become extinct. Sadly, many eligible and propertied young men shied away from the alliance because Ayyappa insisted on okka-parije.

Doddavva herself did not relish the idea of marrying into a clan where she would be treated merely as another daughter-in-law. She would lose all the independence she enjoyed in the Alamanda house. A few years later, during the annual village festival in Armeri, Doddavva met a handsome young man named Uthacha from the well-known Mathanda family. They had several encounters and their friendship soon blossomed into romance.

One day, when Uthacha broached the subject of marriage, Doddavva was forthright and said, 'Yes, but only if you are willing to take on the Alamanda family name.' After momentarily hesitating, Uthacha agreed. When Doddavva announced her choice to her father, he was initially taken by surprise.

'It is the exclusive preserve of the parents to choose the groom,' Ayyappa tried to assert. However, knowing his daughter's single-mindedness, Ayyappa soon gave his consent to the alliance. Luckily, their horoscopes matched. The marriage attracted a great deal of attention since okka-parije was rare. In a special ceremony during the wedding, the elders from Mathanda clan and Ayyappa formally agreed to Uthacha, relinquishing his rights in his family property, and thereby taking on the okka name of his wife's. With okka-parije having been solemnized, the children of Doddavva and Uthacha would be raised as members of Alamanda okka, and would inherit the vast estate.

Uthacha, though a good man, was no match for Doddavva in stature and intelligence. It was widely believed that Doddavva chose Uthacha for this very reason so that she could be in full control of her own destiny. During that period, she was renowned as the strongest, wisest and richest of all Kodava women. Doddavva was what we nowadays refer to as an alpha-female!

After the demise of her father, Doddavva assumed full charge of the property and started looking after every aspect of her estate. Her husband Uthacha functioned more like a manager and took instructions from his domineering wife. Over a period of time, Doddavva earned a great deal of respect and reverence from people across all villages in the southern area of Kodagu. She was generous and lent a helping hand to the needy. Many came to her for her wise counsel on various matters.

With the passage of time Doddavva became the main driving force in Armeri village. At regular intervals caravans of bullock-carts would go to Kannur carrying rice, and on their return trip fetch salt, edible oil, dried fish and other commodities. This business was entirely controlled by Doddavva. She would plan and organize the villagers, the bullock-carts and all the other requirements for the long journey. On occasions, if she found the loading of rice sacks not quick enough, she would just push the men aside, carry a sack in each hand and place them in the carts herself.

Doddavva's fame soon reached Mudduraja in Haleri who controlled most parts of Kodagu during that time. The raja was keen on meeting this great lady. During one of his visits to Armeri, Mudduraja finally got to meet Doddavva. Having heard of her strength, he wanted to see for himself a demonstration of her prowess. When the raja posed this question, Doddavva replied, 'Let us have a contest of hurling a sack of salt.'

In the competition held in honour of the raja, Doddavva heaved a sack full of salt farther than any other man in the village!

Mudduraja discussed various issues concerning administration with Doddavva and was highly impressed by her wisdom and truthfulness. During his extensive rule of fifty-four years, Mudduraja regularly met her whenever he needed advice. In appreciation of Doddavva's wise recommendations, he gifted several acres of land to her and made the Alamanda family the thakkas (headmen) of the village. Even now, the Alamanda family continues to be the thakkas of Armeri village.

In the course of time, Doddavva gave birth to four beautiful daughters. However, she was very much disappointed at not having borne a son and heir to the property. Uthacha and Doddavva faced the same dilemma as her father Ayyappa. The Alamanda family once again encountered the absence of a male heir.

Doddavva's eldest daughter married a member from the Palecanda family, the second daughter was married into the Pulianda family, and the husband of the third daughter was from the Ammanichanda family. The youngest daughter was also betrothed into the Palecanda family. The youngest was Doddavva's favourite daughter. Doddavva came to an understanding with the Palecanda family that she would adopt the sons born to this daughter. Uthacha and Doddavva would raise them as members of the Alamanda family. This practice was known as makka-parije.

Four sons were born to this daughter. Doddavva adopted

two of the boys—Thimmayya and Machayya. In accordance with the practice of makka-parije, Doddavva raised her grandsons Thimmayya and Machayya as members of the Alamanda family. They were the inheritors of the vast estate of Doddavva. Continuing the royal patronage, Thimmayya's son Muddayya was brought up in the Madikeri Palace along with Mudduraja's grandchildren, and was popularly known as Aramane Muddayya. Machayya's great-grandson Alamanda Somayya was the first Kodava to embrace Christianity in 1853 under a programme of proselytizing by the Protestant priest Rev. Hermann Moegling. He was christened Stephanous Somayya, but that's another story.

UTHA NAYAKA

Mudduraja, the third ruler of the Haleri dynasty, looked forward to every Sunday when his subjects brought food-grains, vegetables, fruits, soap-nut powder, kachampuli etc., to his palace at Haleri. His people genuinely loved to fetch for their raja these supplies grown locally in their land. In return, Mudduraja listened to the problems faced by his subjects. Each village took turns in providing the raja and his family their weekly requirements. Mudduraja himself supervised the storage of these provisions in the palace granary. The villagers carried the supplies and they usually had to walk great distances through dense forests. By the end of the day, the raja gave them a hearty meal called 'thombarada oota' prepared in the palace kitchen. An audience was then held where the village headmen presented their petitions to the raja.

A week before Puthari, the harvest festival, during December one year, the privilege of supplying provisions to the palace fell on the people of Beppunad where the Baduvanda family were the desa thakkas, or the village heads. It was considered a matter of great honour for the village to supply groceries to the raja during the festival season. Following the custom, the Baduvanda family organized the consignment to be taken to Haleri. All able-bodied men volunteered to carry the loads. Amongst the group was a tall, strapping, teenaged boy named Utha. Utha was the cowherd of the village. He was a popular lad in Beppunad, and enthusiastically carried out odd jobs entrusted to him by the elders of the village.

During the thombarada oota, Mudduraja joined the people from Beppudnad for the feast. He enquired if all the volunteers were fed well and were satisfied with the meal. During his audience with the village headmen, Mudduraja agreed to build a Kali temple in the village.

The sumptuous meal and weariness of the day caught up with the men and they retired inside the fort for the night. They had to make the long journey back to their village the following day.

The next morning, while the villagers were still fast asleep, a Brahmin named Narasaiah came to the palace as he did every day at daybreak. His job was to give details of rahu kala, gullige kala (the auspicious timings) for any important assignment to be taken up in the palace. He was an astute astrologer as well. Mudduraja consulted Narasaiah before embarking on any major task.

As Narasaiah walked past the group of villagers snoring away during the wee hours of the morning, he noticed the first rays of sun fall on young Utha. The Brahmin found something striking about the boy. Narasaiah walked close to Utha and his sharp eyes caught sight of a unique pattern of a lotus below the boy's right toe. Astrologically, this sign meant that the youth would one day occupy a very powerful position. Narasaiah immediately went inside Mudduraja's chambers and informed the raja of his finding. He requested the raja to retain Utha in the palace so that he could study the boy's horoscope in detail.

Thereafter, Utha was woken up by the guards, and told that he was to remain in the palace as the king wanted to see him. He was terrified as he feared that he had unintentionally committed some grievous crime. Utha pleaded with the soldiers who detained him as just a poor innocent cowherd.

After Mudduraja finished his morning prayers and breakfast, Utha was brought to the court before the raja. 'I want the boy's palm read, and all relevant information collected about his family background, time of birth etc., so that a proper prediction could be made,' Mudduraja instructed Narasaiah. Narasaiah lost no time in gathering all the necessary details that were required. He did lengthy calculations, and crosschecked the data with the voluminous scrolls of manuscripts he carried. After a couple of hours, Narasaiah came back to the court and approached Mudduraja. He whispered to the raja that his study had confirmed his earlier deductions that the boy would rise to be a very powerful individual in the future, and might even become the ruler of his own domain.

Mudduraja had three sons and was very unhappy at this prediction. He feared for the future of his sons and the dynasty. He wanted Narasaiah to tell him if there was any alternative to avert this forecast. Mudduraja urged the astrologer to advise him. Feeling despondent he asked: 'Narasaiah, tell me, should we put the young boy to death immediately to forestall the impending prophesy?'

However, Narasaiah, who had also made a thorough study of the horoscope of the three sons of Mudduraja, assured him that there was no need to panic. 'Mahaswami, there is no need to take such a drastic step. From my study, I am sure your sons will overcome their adversaries and will have a long reign over their dominions.' Narasaiah further advised Mudduraja to keep Utha in the palace and raise him along with his heirs.

This way a close watch could be kept on the boy. It was also possible that Utha might turn out be an able subordinate who could be useful to the raja, and later to the princes when they assumed power.

In a story similar to that of Acchu Nayaka, Utha grew well in the privileged surroundings of the palace and trained along with the princes. Vigorous and strong, he excelled in the use of all weapons as well as in horsemanship. His abilities highly impressed Mudduraja who became quite fond of the boy and started treating him at par with his own sons. Tall and handsome, Utha was admired by the princesses in the palace. However, with the passage of time and the royal patronage, Utha started behaving arrogantly, though he was still highly respectful to Mudduraja. Mudduraja's eldest son, Siribai Veerappa, developed a strong dislike for the headstrong Utha, and did not relish his father treating the village boy as part of the family.

By the time Utha was twenty-five, he had proved to be an asset to Mudduraja. Utha took part in several campaigns of the raja, and shouldered great responsibilities. He demonstrated unquestioned loyalty to the raja. So impressed was Mudduraja with Utha, that he not only set aside the prophecy, but also gave his daughter Neelammaji in marriage to him. Utha had already converted to the Lingayat sect when he was adopted by the raja to live in the palace. Having gained the confidence of Mudduraja, Utha one day requested his father-in-law, 'Please give me the responsibility of administering my village in Beppunad. I will strengthen your rule in the southern parts of Kodagu.' Mudduraja readily consented and conferred the title of nayaka on him.

This appointment of Utha as a nayaka created a great deal

of heartburn to some of the elders in Beppunad who had seen Utha grow up as a cowherd in their village. The members of Baduvanda family, who were the desa thakkas, were especially resentful of Utha Nayaka and his supercilious behaviour. They could not reconcile themselves to the arrogance displayed by Utha.

A highfalutin Utha, now son-in-law of the king, expected his old village folks including the elders to pay obeisance to him. When this was not forthcoming, he was furious and took violent revenge on his own people. He set ablaze the Ainmane of Iychettira and Bachettira clans, and these families barely managed to survive. Nervous of approaching Mudduraja, the thakkas from the Baduvanda family made a representation to Utha's brother-in-law Siribai Veerappa, regarding the highhandedness of Utha. Veerappa tried to advise Utha not to be harsh, and urged him to treat his people with compassion. But it was all in vain. Utha was apathetic and continued his imperiousness. Over-confident of himself, he subtly started scheming against Veerappa, the heir-apparent of Mudduraja. For a while, it seemed as though Narasaiah's astrological prediction that had alarmed Mudduraja, was being made feasible by the raja himself.

Around this time, Mudduraja died and Siribai Veerappa ascended the throne of Kodagu. Without Mudduraja's patronage, Utha now felt threatened. He clandestinely started conniving with Kotangadi Veeravarma who ruled the neighbouring Wynad area in Kerala, to overthrow Veerappa. Utha also befriended Acchu Nayaka in Anchigeri and tried to form an alliance against his brother-in-law.

Soon, Utha built a strong army of loyal supporters, and attempted to unite the Kodavas against Siribai Veerappa. An opportunistic Utha now identified himself with the Kodavas and rallied them against the Lingayat rulers. Acchu Nayaka also extended his support to Utha and, on his instigation, refused to pay tribute to the Haleri raja. During Mudduraja's reign, Utha had overshadowed Siribai Veerappa. Some of the local chieftains saw an opportunity to reinforce their power by defying the new raja whose capabilities were yet to be tested. Utha's ambition made him turn against the family of his benefactor. Siribai Veerappa was furious with Utha whom he called a traitor, and swore to eliminate him.

SIRIBAI VEERAPPA RAJA

Mudduraja always remembered what his grandfather Veeraraja said to him while he sat on his lap as a child: 'My Muddu, one day you will become the king of this dynasty started by me. Have high aspirations, and instill the same qualities in your children and grandchildren.'

Mudduraja was a young man of twenty when his father Appajiraja suddenly passed away. As soon as he ascended the throne, he set out on expanding his influence in Kodagu. Mudduraja believed in winning the hearts and minds of people. He abhorred the use of the sword. By the time he was forty years old, he was popularly accepted as the raja of Kodagu, and all the nayakas paid homage to him.

It was around this time that a son was born to his royal consort. While there was great rejoicing at the birth of an heir, Mudduraja was shocked and devastated to find that his first-born had a physical deformity. The child was siribai, or hare-lipped. He summoned his trusted astrologer Narasaiah to check the horoscope of his son. The learned Brahmin took a week to make a detailed study. He then came to the anxious raja and announced: 'You have no reasons to worry Mahaswami. Your son is a siribai, which is a sign of good fortune and greatness. He will overcome all obstacles, and rule a larger territory than you do.' Mudduraja and his wife were greatly relieved by this forecast. They named the child Veerappa, who was later popularly known to his subjects and adversaries alike as Siribai Veerappa Raja.

When the fifty-four-year reign of Mudduraja ended in 1687, Veerappa succeeded him as the ruler at the new capital established at Madikeri. Mudduraja had provided a jagir or landlordship for his two younger sons. His second son Appajiraja settled in Haleri Palace, and the youngest son Nandaraja was given a palace at Horamale in Gallibedu near Madikeri.

Veerappa had gained valuable experience in statecraft as heir-apparent of Mudduraja. He had also taken part in a few battles during his father's reign. However, as soon as he became the king, threats of invasions loomed large over his domain from Mysore in the east and Kerala in the south. To add to his woes, there was internal dissension spearheaded by his brother-in-law Utha Nayaka.

Chikka Devaraja Wodeyar was on the throne of Mysore at that time. He was a highly ambitious ruler and was bent on conquering the neighbouring areas. Periapatna, which was ruled by Nanjaraja, a distant relative of the Haleri dynasty, soon fell to the Mysore army. Chikka Devaraja Wodeyar had already added Coimbatore and the surrounding areas to his kingdom. He then turned his attention towards Kodagu. A strong army was sent to invade Kodagu. They crossed the border through the eastern margin at Balele and camped at the plains of Palpare. Veerappa, forewarned of the invasion, planned a surprise pre-dawn attack on the Mysore army. His well-trained army of Kodavas fell on the startled intruders and, in a hand-to-hand combat, massacred nearly 15,000 enemy soldiers. The survivors were subsequently chased well out of the boundaries of Kodagu.

Around the same time, Kotangadi Veeravarma, who ruled Wynad in Kerala plotted an invasion on Kodagu from the south. He tried to take advantage of Siribai Veerappa Raja's preoccupation with the attack from Mysore. Veeravarma had an ally in Kodagu, namely Utha Nayaka, who had fallen out with his brother-in-law Siribai Veerappa. Veeravarma moved into Kodagu with a 5,000 strong army of Nairs, and camped in an improvised garrison in the dense forest near the village Tomara. Utha Nayaka assured Veeravarma, 'I will provide you supply of food, and support you with my followers to defeat Veerappa.'

On hearing about the incursion of the Kerala forces into his territory, Veerappa despatched a 1,500 strong posse of Kodavas to lay siege on the fortress put up by Veeravarma. On hearing of Utha Nayaka's collusion with Veeravarma, his childhood dislike for him intensified. Consequently, he had all the supply routes to the fort cut-off. After a few days, the invaders were left hopelessly in shortage of food. By then, Veerappa had successfully warded off the attack from the Mysore raja. Brimming with confidence after their victory against Mysore, Veerappa and his men came over to Tomara to settle scores with Veeravarma and Utha Nayaka. Sensing the dire consequences of his deceit, Utha Nayaka abandoned Veeravarma and fled to the forest. Veeravarma on the other hand was stranded, and tried desperately to make peace with Veerappa. But Siribai Veerappa was determined to teach him a lesson. The Kodagu army led by Veerappa Raja stormed the temporary fortifications of Veeravarma, and the intruder's demoralized men were mercilessly killed. Veeravarma surrendered and pleaded for mercy, but Veerappa had him brutally executed.

Thereafter, Veerappa sent his men to capture the treacherous Utha Nayaka. He denounced Utha Nayaka for being ungrateful to the Haleri dynasty after having enjoyed the privileges bestowed on him by Veerappa's father, Mudduraja. Utha Nayaka initially sought refuge with his friend Anchigeri Acchu Nayaka but when Veerappa's men came in hot pursuit, he fled to Baithur in Kerala with his family. He ultimately died a disappointed man in poverty. Years later, some of his family members returned to Kodagu and established the Nayakanda family in Beppunad.

Veerappa had to contend with a few more dissidents within Kodagu. Anchigeri's Acchu Nayaka and Kollakongi Nayaka continued to defy Siribai Veerappa's authority and refused to pay any tribute. In 1718, he entrusted the task of eliminating these two nayakas to his trusted commander Kariakara Paradanda Ponnappa.

Paradanda Ponnappa was a seasoned warrior. He took hundred able-bodied Kodava soldiers and camped in a village near Kollakongi Nayaka's stronghold. The attack was efficiently planned and was carried out early in the morning.

Taking their adversaries by surprise, they gained access to the fort. In the battle that followed, Ponnappa and his men overpowered and killed Kollakongi Nayaka, his brothers and several other soldiers.

Next, Kariakara Ponnappa devised an elaborate stratagem to eliminate the powerful Acchu Nayaka. He and five of his men disguised themselves as mendicants and stalked the strong fortification of Acchu Nayaka in Anchigeri village. They spent several days in and out of Anchigeri and collected crucial information from the villagers. Acchu Nayaka got the news of Kollakongi Nayaka's defeat and subsequent death. He anticipated an imminent attack from Veerappa, and took all precautions to strengthen his defence. He expanded the kadangas and posted sentries at all approaches leading to his domain. However, when there was no sign of any hostile movement towards his region even after about fifteen days, he relaxed and let his guard down.

It was a good time of the year to go on a hunt. Acchu Nayaka, being fond of shikar, set out with a large retinue leaving just a handful of soldiers to guard the fort. Ponnappa, who was keeping a close watch, chose this opportune moment for a sudden strike. He knew that the hunting party would not get back before late in the night. Ponnappa quietly encircled the village with his men and with about twenty able-bodied soldiers, approached the fort from the backyard. Under the cover of darkness, they stealthily climbed the high walls and got entry into the fort. Two men were left behind to warn the return of the hunting party. A few of the guards inside the fort were sleeping and were taken unawares. They fell to the odikathis of Ponnappa's men. The women inside the fort got wind of the intruders, but kept quiet, locked in their rooms waiting for Acchu Nayaka and his men to return. By the time the hunting party got back, it was well past ten in the night. The hunt was good and Acchu's men were happy and tired. Ponnappa's soldiers disguised as Acchu's men opened the front gate of the fort and let Acchu and his men enter. As they were unloading the spoils of the hunt, the women let out shrill alarms informing of the intruders inside the fort. Swords were drawn and a vicious fight erupted. Ponnappa's men hiding in the forest too joined in. Ponnappa engaged Acchu Nayaka in close combat and it soon became a one-on-one fight between the two able warriors. They asked their fighters to stand aside and challenged each other.

After a while, Ponnappa overpowered Acchu Nayaka who was grievously hurt with a deep gash on his head. In the attack, most of Acchu's men were killed and Acchu Nayaka was taken prisoner. Ponnappa stayed on in Acchu's fort for two weeks till he and Acchu Nayaka recovered from their injuries. Following the defeat, the people of Anchigeri surrendered to Veerappa and accepted him as their ruler. Acchu Nayaka was then taken to Madikeri and presented before Siribai Veerappa Raja.

Veerappa received Acchu Nayaka with all the respects due to a leader. He admired the gallant Acchu, but kept him and his family under house arrest in Madikeri lest he regroup his supporters and pose a threat to him again. The free-spirited Acchu wilted in captivity. He was deeply distressed at his people having to be subservient to a dynasty foreign to Kodagu. Within a couple of years, his health deteriorated and he died. After Acchu's death, his son went over to Kerala where he learnt tantra, the practice of occult. He returned to Kodagu after several years and became influential as a practitioner of tantra. He started a family, which is the prominent Ajjikuttira clan of today.

Paradanda Ponnappa and his men received well-deserved rewards from Veerappa Raja for eliminating his powerful adversaries. Veerappa Raja's dominance was now well-established all over Kodagu. Ponnappa was rewarded with large tracts of paddy lands conquered from Kollakongi Nayaka, and areas of land that originally belonged to the decimated Mukkatira family in Kunjalageri village. Paradanda Ponnappa was elevated to the position of dewan after these successful missions. He later settled in Kunjalageri village and named his family Mukkatira okka.

After Siribai Veerappa vanquished the rival nayakas, he succeeded in bringing all of Kodagu and some of the territories in Sullya, under the absolute rule of the Haleri dynasty. He streamlined the administration and divided Kodagu into twelve kombus and thirty-five nads or villages. Prominent Kodavas were appointed as village chiefs known as thakkas, who had powers to adjudicate in any dispute between villagers in their areas. These were ranked as seme-thakkas, ooru-thakkas, and desa-thakkas. There is an interesting account as to how the kombus were demarcated. It seems, that a horn-shaped brass trumpet known as kombu would be blown, and the distance to which it could be heard would be marked in four directions. This area was designated as a kombu!

Siribai Veerappa ruled for forty-nine years. He was, however, not happy with the conduct of his only son, Appajiraja (named after his grandfather). His resentment against his son was so intense that he declared Appajiraja unfit to rule after him. Siribai Veerappa was annoyed at his promiscuous son, who showed no interest in learning statecraft. Appajiraja had also caused the death of his principal wife at the instigation of one of his mistresses. A furious and uncompromising Veerappa threw Appajiraja along with his infant son, Chikka Veerappa, in jail. Appajiraja died in prison after twelve years of incarceration. Siribai Veerappa, now a septuagenarian, was finally persuaded by his noblemen to name his grandson Chikka Veerappa as his successor since the boy had committed no crime and had been unfairly punished. A mellowed Veerappa acquiesced, and Chikka Veerappa was personally crowned as king by his grandfather. Siribai Veerappa died in 1736 at the age of seventy-eight. Two of his consorts committed sati by jumping into his funeral pyre.

HYDER ALI AND TIPU SULTAN IN COORG

In June 1761, Hyder Ali, who was one of the army commanders of the raja of Mysore, usurped power after overthrowing the weak king Chikka Krishnaraja Wodeyar. Thereafter, he took full control of the strategic fort in Srirangapatna, imprisoned the royal family, and also crowned himself as the Nawab of Mysore.

Soon after he established his rule over Mysore, he set out to expand his newly acquired domain and conquered most of the territories in the neighbouring areas controlled by paleygars and nayakas. He defeated the Ikkeri nayakas and annexed their provinces to his realm, which extended up to Mangalore. Hyder Ali, however, did not plan an immediate adventure against Kodagu. He was well aware of the crushing defeat suffered by the army of Mysore under Chikka Devaraja Wodeyar, during the reign of Siribai Veerappa. Nevertheless, he kept making various demands on Chikka Veerappa who had succeeded his grandfather on the throne of Kodagu.

In the summer of 1765, Hyder Ali deputed his commander Fazal-ulla-Khan to lay claim on some of the provinces in the disputed Yelusaviraseme (land of seven thousand hamlets) in the north of Kodagu. This led to several skirmishes, but Kodagu forces were successful in thwarting Hyder's attempts. Hyder Ali, on the advice of his dewan and mentor Purnayya, made a cunning proposal to the raja of Kodagu to end the hostilities.

Kodagu would get one of the villages, Uchangi, near Kodlipet, for a payment of three lakh rupees. He wanted half the amount to be paid immediately, and offered the village to be occupied by the raja of Kodagu. In order to ensure the balance payment, Hyder Ali wanted a written assurance, and a prominent person as hostage from Kodagu. Chikka Veerappa, keen on avoiding further clashes, agreed to the proposal and sent one of his commanders, Bonira Charmanna, to Srirangapatna along with the initial payment.

However, before Chikka Veerappa could take possession of Uchangi, he suddenly died in 1766 without an heir. His death ended the lineage of Siribai Veerappa.

In a rare case of perfect harmony, Mudduraja II of Haleri and his cousin Muddayyaraja from the Horamale branch of the family jointly ruled Kodagu from 1766 to 1770. With the change at the helm, Hyder Ali deliberately ignored to honour his promise of ceding Uchangi village to Kodagu. Mudduraja II and Muddayyaraja reminded Hyder Ali to keep his pledge and transfer the village to their dominion but Hyder Ali wanted the balance amount to be paid first. The rajas of Kodagu, suspected foul play and deputed Mudduraja's able brother Lingaraja to deal with Fazal-ulla-Khan who was camping in Yelusaviraseme. Fighting soon broke out and Lingaraja waged a spirited attack on the Mysore forces competently assisted by his commanders, Kananda Doddayya and Appachara Mandanna. The Kodagu army was victorious and Lingaraja chased Fazal-ulla-Khan down the Besele ghats towards south Kanara. However, the two gallant Kodava commanders, Kananda Doddayya and Appachara Mandanna, lost their lives in the fighting. In the meantime, in Srirangapatna, Bonira Charmanna died of smallpox. Subsequently, Hyder Ali saw the futility in fighting the indomitable Kodagu forces. He sought friendship with the rajas of Kodagu, and in lieu of Uchangi, agreed to cede two villages near Amar-Sullya, namely Panje and Ballare. This arrangement was accepted and there were no further hostilities between Mysore and Kodagu for a while.

In 1770, the joint rule of Mudduraja II and Muddayyaraja came to an abrupt end when both the rajas died within a short span of time. An internecine family dispute over succession forced Lingaraja, the influential brother of Mudduraja II, to flee Kodagu. In an ironic twist, he sought refuge with Hyder Ali in Mysore along with his three sons and nephew Appajiraja, the son of Mudduraja II. Muddayyaraja's son Mallayya mustered sufficient support to hoist his son Devapparaja on the throne in 1770. Out of desperation, Lingaraja unwisely sought the help of Hyder Ali to resolve the dispute. The Nawab of Mysore was overjoyed at this golden opportunity to directly meddle in the affairs of Kodagu.

In 1773, Hyder Ali helped Lingaraja to invade Kodagu. Many Kodava supporters of Lingaraja joined forces with him. Unable to face the attack, Devapparaja moved out of Kodagu. Fearing for his life, he travelled in disguise and reached the banks of Tungabhadra in Dharwar. Betrayed by informants, Devapparaja and his family soon fell into the hands of Hyder Ali's soldiers and were brought to Srirangapatna. In 1774, Hyder Ali put him and his entire family to death with the tacit approval of Lingaraja. This extinguished the Horamale branch of the Haleri dynasty.

Gaining a foothold in Kodagu, Hyder Ali demanded an annual tribute of 24,000 rupees from Lingaraja, who now sat on the throne of Kodagu. Nonetheless, the Nawab of Mysore appointed his own administrators for Kodagu and treated Lingaraja as a vassal. Lingaraja resisted the total takeover of Kodagu by Hyder Ali, which led to his strained relationship with the Nawab of Mysore. Lingaraja's bravery on the battlefield had earned him great admiration and loyalty from the Kodavas. But when Lingaraja suddenly died in 1780, leaving behind three minor sons, Kodavas were alarmed and concerned about the future of the kingdom. They feared Hyder Ali's evil designs on Kodagu. In a deft move, Hyder Ali took charge of the three princes and the rest of the royal family under the pretext of playing guardian, but in effect made them prisoners. He would have annexed Kodagu to Mysore had the British not attacked his territories in Arcot. While fighting the British in Arcot, Hyder Ali developed a cancerous growth termed as 'king's ulcer' on his back, and died as a result of it in 1782.

Taking advantage of this situation, the people of Kodagu revolted against the administrators of Hyder Ali and laid siege to the Madikeri Fort, where a military garrison was stationed. After Tipu succeeded his father, he made no pretensions about the imprisonment of Lingaraja's three sons: Veerarajendra, Appajiraja and Lingarajendra, at the old fort in Periapatna. Along with the princes, a daughter of late Lingaraja and two daughters of his brother Mudduraja II were also taken as hostages. The revolt was, however, quickly put down by Mysore forces and the Kodavas were subdued.

In March 1785, Tipu Sultan marched through Kodagu on his way from Mangalore to Mysore. He had just signed a reconciliatory pact 'The Mangalore Treaty' with the British after his victorious Second Anglo-Mysore war. He tried to win over the people of Kodagu by pardoning them for revolting against him and his father on seven different occasions. When the response was muted, he warned them of dire consequences if they defied his control over the land. He berated the Kodavas for leading an immoral life and threatened to convert them to Islam. He also enraged the Kodavas by accusing them of practicing polyandry.

Soon, Kodagu plunged into turmoil again. Kodavas resisted Tipu's rule and were determined to fight for the release of the heir to the throne, Veerarajendra, and his family. They waged relentless guerrilla warfare on Tipu's army. In August 1785, Tipu despatched 15,000 soldiers under the command of Janulabin. 4,000 Kodavas, led by their chieftains, launched a well-coordinated attack on Tipu's army at Ulagulli near Sunticoppal. Janulabin lost thousands of his men and was forced to retreat to Bettadapura.

Within two months, Tipu himself descended on Coorg with a formidable army which included some French soldiers, and camped at Ulagulli for six weeks. In the meantime, Janulabin joined forces from Bettadapura. In the ensuing battle, many Kodavas lost their lives. Tipu entered Madikeri and again made conciliatory gestures towards the Kodava chieftains to end the hostilities. But Kodavas distrusted Tipu and feared for the safety of their women and children. They were also wary of Tipu's threats to convert them to Islam.

After fifteen days in Madikeri, Tipu moved close to Tala-Kavery and camped in a vast open area. With the promise of reconciliation, he lured thousands of poor Kodavas from nearby villages for negotiation. Their leaders were deliberately kept out. The worst fears of the Kodavas came true when his troops suddenly seized the Kodavas along with women and children. They were forcibly taken by foot to Srirangapatna. As a result, many perished on the way. On reaching Srirangapatna, all the men were forcibly converted to Islam. They were given military training and made sepoys in his army. The converted Kodava soldiers were given uniforms with tiger stripes, and their regiment was named as Ahamedi. In celebration of this large addition to Islam, Tipu declared himself as 'Badshah' to rival the Mughals in Delhi.

Tipu strengthened the Madikeri Fort by replacing the mud walls with bulwarks of stone, and stationed his trusted Lieutenant Jaffar Kulli Baig with additional forces, well-armed to impose his writ on Kodagu. He renamed Madikeri as Jaffarabad. He also reinforced the forts at Beppunad, Kushalnagar, and Bagamandala. In Bagamandala, which he renamed as Abjalabad, the temple itself was taken over and converted into a garrison. The Brahmin priests secretly took away the idols from the temple, kept them safely in the forest, and continued with the regular poojas. Tipu appointed his faithful aide Janulabin, as the administrator of Kodagu.

Both Hyder Ali and Tipu Sultan had recognized the strategic importance of Kodagu for defence against attacks on Mysore from the west coast since the Western Ghats offered a vantage point to prevent strikes from the west. Thus, Tipu Sultan was hell-bent on subduing the Kodavas and in building a strong defence on the Western Ghats to safeguard his domain from the growing threat from the British East India Company.

A KINGDOM NEARLY LOST

It was dusk. In the fading light, the seventeen-year-old Veerarajendra was preoccupied teaching his younger brothers—Appajiraja and Lingarajendra—the art of using the Coorg knife or the odi-kathi. He was impressed with the seven-year-old Lingarajendra's proficiency with the odi-kathi—a broad-bladed knife ideal for close combat. He found the rather squat and dusky boy quite adept at using the spear as well. On the other hand, ten-year-old Appajiraja was well-built and handsome, but a trifle conceited. Just then, one of the guards who brought in the oil-soaked torch sidled up to Veerarajendra and whispered the news of unrest in Madikeri. They were at the far corner of the old palace at Haleri built by their ancestors. It had been their home for over a year. Veerarajendra and his family were confined in the rundown palace since the demise of his father Lingaraja in February 1780. His people were unhappy and angry that Hyder Ali had appointed a Brahmin as administrator while Veerarajendra, the rightful heir to the throne, was kept confined in remote Haleri. Initially, Hyder Ali had given the impression that young Veerarajendra and other members of the family needed his protection, and with this in mind, he was keeping them out of danger.

Veerarajendra was witness to his father's struggle in wresting control of Kodagu. He had acquired wisdom beyond his years, and was well aware of Hyder Ali's intentions. His

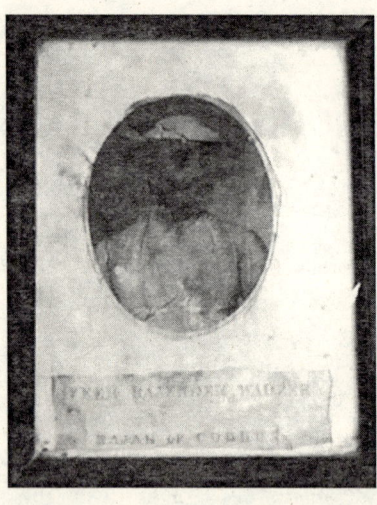

Veerarajendra

father Lingaraja had secured the throne of Kodagu with the help of the Nawab. In return for this favour, Lingaraja had to accept a protectorate status for Kodagu under Hyder Ali. He paid an annual tribute of 24,000 rupees to the new ruler of Mysore. However, despite their superior fighting force, the Mysore army was unable to subjugate Lingaraja and his Kodava fighters. It was an uneasy peace. Now, with the death of the Lingaraja, Hyder Ali believed that it was an appropriate time to wrest total control of Kodagu and tactfully sideline the popular Haleri dynasty of the Lingayat rajas.

Hyder Ali was on a military campaign in Kerala when he received news of revolt in Kodagu. His mission in Wynad was successful and he was in high spirits. He was further elated at his son Tipu's gallant actions in the Deccan where they were realizing their aim of expanding their realm. Hyder knew that in a few days the monsoon would lash across the Western Ghats and fighting the highlanders would be extremely difficult. He decided on crushing the unrest immediately and decisively. He moved his mighty fighting force up the Perambadi Ghats to Kodagu and was ruthless in quelling the rebellion. As an incentive, he offered five rupees to his soldiers for every severed head of Kodava warriors. There was total carnage, and after a while Hyder Ali himself was appalled at the massacre. He had to personally intervene to stop further bloodshed when he saw severed heads of young boys his troops brought to claim their reward. Most of the Coorgs who survived fled to the mountains and forests.

To prevent further attempts by the citizens at rallying behind young Veerarajendra, the rightful heir, Hyder Ali deported the royal family out of Kodagu to faraway Gorur in Arakalgod. Veerarajendra's wife Nanjammaji, mother Devambika, sister Neelammaji and two cousins were also kept under virtual house arrest in the dingy old fort at Gorur. He appointed one of his subordinates, Hombale Nayaka, an influential Vokkaliga leader, to oversee and chaperon the royal family. The Nawab of Mysore and his son Tipu Sultan basked in their success over Kodagu.

The euphoria over the suppression of the Kodava revolt was short-lived and Hyder Ali and Tipu could not savour their success for long. By late 1781, the British had started making aggressive forays in the Madras region, and Hyder Ali had to move to Arcot to defend his territories. Within months, he fell seriously ill and died in Arcot in 1782. Well-prepared to take on the responsibilities, Hyder Ali's twenty-two-year-old son Tipu Sultan succeeded him as the ruler of Mysore.

During this period of transition, people of Kodagu took

advantage of the preoccupation of the Mysore army against the British, and revolted once again. This time they were led by Kodava chieftains—Kuletira Ponnanna and his brother Machayya. Kodava leaders also made plans to free Veerarajendra from captivity but Tipu got wind of these schemes. In early 1785, he shifted the royal family from Gorur to Periapatna. There he kept them in the sixteenth-century fort built by the Chengalvas since it was better protected by his forces. He appointed one of his lieutenants, Ismail Khan, to assist Hombale Nayaka in guarding the royal family. Within months of their arrival at Periapatna, tragedy struck the royal family. Veerarajendra's mother Devambika died of smallpox.

By this time, he had conquered most of the neighbouring areas and was supremely confident of himself. His success at the Second Anglo-Mysore War had made him imperious. Then one day he came visiting to the fort at Periapatna. He summoned all the members of the royal family of Kodagu for an audience with him. Thereafter, Tipu addressed Veerarajendra as if he was a vassal. He spoke insultingly and demanded that Veerarajendra and his brothers embrace Islam and spread the faith amongst their subjects in Kodagu. Hombale Nayaka, who was present, was shocked and baulked at this proposal. The twenty-two-year-old heir to the throne sternly replied, 'We would all rather die than give up our religion.' This exchange of heated words led to murmuring in the makeshift court. Sensing displeasure amongst his Hindu supporters, Tipu did not pursue the sensitive issue further.

Consequently, Tipu's eyes fell on Veerarajendra's attractive sister Neelammaji and cousin Devammaji. The following day, he announced that both the teenaged princesses would join his zenana in Srirangapatna, ignoring strong protests from the royal family. Neelammaji's name was changed to Mehatab (half-moon) and Devammaji was renamed Abtab (sun). This action alienated a large number of his Hindu subjects in the domain. Hombale Nayaka was infuriated since he had fallen in love with Neelammaji. Some of the Muslims too sympathized with the royalty of Kodagu. Tipu was tolerant of other faiths only when the citizens accepted his rule without resistance. He threw his secular credentials to the winds when there was any opposition to his authority. When news of Tipu's transgressions reached the people of Kodagu, they were incensed. Tipu had already deeply hurt the Kodavas and other communities by abducting nearly eighty-thousand of their men, women, and children. These atrocities gave further impetus to their determination in fighting against Tipu Sultan's rule and freeing their young heir to the throne.

In the ensuing years, Tipu consolidated his position further. As threats of enemy attacks faded, security around the fort in Periapatna became lax. In December 1788, two prominent Kodava leaders—Pattacheravanda Boluka and Appaneravanda Achayya—secretly hatched a plan to rescue their legitimate king, Veerarajendra, from captivity. Periapatna was a bustling trading town, and villagers from neighbouring areas thronged this town for their groceries and other requirements. Boluka dressed himself as a vendor of coconut oil and started moving around in the vicinity of the fort. One day, on the pretext of selling oil, he gained entry into the fort where there were also a number of other dwellings. He managed to get close to the house where members of the royal family of Kodagu were confined. He befriended one of the guards, and with his help got an audience with Veerarajendra. He elaborated on a plan and subsequently fixed a date for the escape. It was to be on the midnight of 14 December 1788. After Tipu's most undiplomatic handling of the royal family, Hombale Nayaka distanced himself from the Tiger of Mysore. He joined the conspiracy to free Veerarajendra and his family. A disgruntled Ismail Khan too supported the escape plans.

On the moonless night of 14 December, Hombale Nayaka arranged for a special dinner for the royal detainees at their dwelling inside the fort. In a gesture of fake magnanimity, he invited the guards who were shivering outside in the cold, to partake in the feast. A liberal sprinkling of dope was added to their meal. Within an hour, the guards were blissfully asleep.

Pattacheravanda Boluka and Appaneravanda Achayya were waiting outside the fort along with ten able-bodied men. A rope ladder was lowered into the fort and one by one the royal family climbed out of their captivity. Veerarajendra carried on his back his slender wife Nanjammaji, who had recently given birth to a baby girl named Rajammaji. His brother Appajiraja carried the eight-month-old baby. Hombale Nayaka carried the youngest brother Lingarajendra.

Once outside the fort, they had to pass through a colony of guards. Nanjammaji and Lingarajendra were carried by two strong men, in large wicker baskets, meant for coconut oil containers. The rest walked without making any noise. Just then, the little infant in the hands of Appajiraja started crying. A few dogs barked, and it would have been a matter of minutes before the guards were alerted. Veerarajendra, out of sheer desperation, signalled Ismail Khan to strangle and silence the child.

Ismail Khan immediately took the child in his arms and

gestured to everyone to keep moving. He was in the habit of chewing opium. He took a small shard of the drug, wetted it in his mouth, and fed it to the infant. The child immediately fell into deep slumber.

In the pitch-dark night, they hurried through the thickets, unmindful of injuries, scratches and bruises from slipping and falling. It took well over two hours for them to reach the border of Kodagu. A large contingency of Veerarajendra's supporters was eagerly waiting for their raja and his family with palanquins and horses. As soon as Nanjammaji was lowered and got out of the basket, the first question she asked was, 'Where is my little Rajammaji?' Veerarajendra took her aside and broke the news of the harsh action he had to take of sacrificing the child for the sake of rest of the family. Nanjammaji was inconsolable.

Just then, Ismail Khan came up to Veerarajendra and said, 'Raja, I have a confession to make. I disobeyed your orders.' He gently unwrapped the cloth in which he had bundled little Rajammaji, who was still fast asleep. Veerarajendra and his wife were ecstatic. They profusely thanked Ismail Khan and Hombale Nayaka. Veerarajendra promised them grant of land, and senior positions in the court once he was on the throne of Kodagu.

Kodavas came out of their retreat in the mountains and rallied behind their young and energetic raja. Veerarajendra started taking control of one village after another. In June 1789, Veerarajendra deputed his trusted Kariakara, Kuletira Ponnanna, to capture Tipu's fort at Kushalnagar. Ponnanna attacked the fort with an army of 1,500 men, and after intense fighting succeeded in chasing the enemy across river Kavery. He triumphantly brought the head of Tipu's commander at the fort as a trophy for Veerarajendra.

In August 1789, Tipu's garrison at Armeri in Beppunad was overrun by Veerarajendra's army. In February 1790, Veerarajendra bombarded the Bagamandala temple complex with cannon fire, which was being used as a fort by Tipu's soldiers. The occupiers surrendered after two days of resistance. When they beseeched for mercy, the raja gave them safe passage out of Kodagu. Large stock of arms and ammunition were captured from Tipu's army.

Following the recapture of the Bagamandala temple, the priests returned from their hiding with the idols. The temple was consecrated once again. Veerarajendra replaced the two copper tiles on the roof of the temple, damaged during the shelling, with silver tiles. These silver tiles can be observed now by those who visit this holy place. There are a few evidences of destruction of some of the stone statues near the temple.

By 1791, Veerarajendra captured the important and strategic Madikeri Fort along with a large cache of arms and ammunition, and re-established the Haleri dynasty's rule over Kodagu. Jaffar Beg surrendered to him and pleaded for his life. A magnanimous Veerarajendra provided Jaffar and his men escorts to return to Mysore without getting molested by the angry citizens of Kodagu.

Thus, Veerarajendra, popularly referred to as Dodda Veerarajendra, was baptized by fire so to speak, before his well-earned ascension to the throne of Kodagu.

VEERARAJENDRA'S ESCAPADES AND A BRIEF HISTORY OF VIRAJPET

Soon after Veerarajendra's escape from Tipu's prison in Periapatna in 1788, he started mobilizing his supporters to evict Tipu's forces entrenched in various fortifications within his kingdom. He settled his family temporarily at Kurchi village in the southern part of Kodagu. Veerarajendra was constantly on the move to foil Tipu's attempts at recapturing him. During this period, the young raja was tricked by an adversary into believing that Palle Veeravarma, the raja of Kote, in neighbouring Wynad would help him in his fight against Tipu. Kote Raja invited Veerarajendra to his territory for a meeting to discuss strategies. Once Veerarajendra crossed the border of Kodagu, he was escorted to Arala village in Wynad. Veerarajendra was made to wait for twenty days, and when Kote Raja finally arrived, he aggressively demanded that Veerarajendra sign a document conceding large parts of southern Kodagu to him.

A trapped Veerarajendra had no choice but to sign the document in exchange for a free passage back to Kodagu.

Palle Veeravarma warned Veerarajendra that this was one of the actions taken by him to avenge the killing of his forefather Kotangadi Veeravarma by Siribai Veerappa of the Haleri dynasty more than a century ago at Tomara.

On his return to Kurchi, Veerarajendra was concerned about the hostile stance of Kote Raja, and feared for the safety of his family. He moved his principal wife Nanjammaji and daughter Rajammaji to a village in Nalaknad. Two of his minor wives and some close family members still remained in Kurchi. In the meantime, Palle Veeravarma made an incursion into Kodagu. However, Veerarajendra with the help of his trusted and able Kodava chieftains, Appaneravanda Achayya and Pattacheravanda Boluka, was able to mobilize sufficient forces to ward off the intruder. A few days later, Palle Veeravarma's spies informed him that Veerarajendra was away from Kurchi, leaving part of his family there. Bent on revenge, the Kote Raja sent his soldiers to ransack Veerarajendra's house. They not only vandalized the dwelling but also brutally massacred all the residents. Veerarajendra was shattered by this incident. He hurriedly fortified his borders to prevent any further intrusions. Unable to take on another foe, he prayed for divine retribution on his enemies.

Veerarajendra gradually gained control over his kingdom village by village. By early 1791, he had ousted Tipu's soldiers from three of the four fortifications. Luckily for the young king, Tipu Sultan's attention was diverted as he was busy fighting the British. For his safety and that of his family, Veerarajendra started building a palace in a remote forested area in Nalaknad, surrounded by natural barriers and well-protected from enemy attacks. The modest palace was completed in a few months and he moved into his new abode with his family in December 1791. The palace was further fortified with a deep moat and high mud walls. By then, he was successful in taking control of the last bastion of Tipu at the fort in Madikeri.

The British realized the strategic importance of Kodagu in their fight against Tipu. In a historic meeting in October

1790 with Robert Taylor, the English Resident at Tellicherry, Veerarajendra and the East India Company signed a formal treaty of friendship—with God, Sun, Moon, and Earth bearing witnesses! This alliance was forged to cooperate in their fight against their common enemy—Tipu Sultan, who had formed a partnership with the topiwallas or the French.

Within months of signing the treaty, the British requested Veerarajendra passage through Kodagu for reinforcement from Bombay via Tellicherry, on their way to Srirangapatna. The raja was also requested to provide food and shelter to the British troops and arrange transport for supplies to be taken to Srirangapatna. Veerarajendra personally received the British troops under the command of General Robert Abercrombie in April 1791. He again met the general at the same spot on his way back to Bombay after an uneasy peace treaty was signed between the British and Tipu Sultan in 1792, at the end of the Third Anglo-Mysore War.

During the second sojourn, General Abercrombie and Veerarajendra had sufficient time to discuss various subjects of mutual interest. General Abercrombie had a flair for languages and could converse in Hindustani and Kannada. Consequently, the young raja and the general became good friends. Veerarajendra wanted a supply of swords, cannons and muskets from the British whereas the general wanted to know about the exotic spices grown in this mountainous terrain. He was also intrigued by the history of the Haleri dynasty. General Abercrombie suggested that Veerarajendra should record the antecedents of his forefathers for posterity. The raja replied, 'I need to secure my kingdom and bring peace and stability to my people before taking up that task.'

After the second meeting with General Abercrombie, Veerarajendra decided to establish a settlement in the area to commemorate the historic solidarity with the British. He named the place as Veerarajendrapette. In May 1792, he ordered the construction of a small fort and an ammunition dump on a hillock. A large pond was also constructed towards the south of this fort for his elephants and horses, which is still in existence and has a perennial supply of water. Later, a makeshift palace was constructed within the fortification. The only remnant of the fort visible at present is the entrance gate with sentry boxes on either side built in lime mortar.

The gate posts at Virajpet

The frequent clashes with Tipu Sultan during 1780s and the abduction of a large number of men, women and children, had depleted the population of Kodagu. The hostages were taken to Srirangapatna and forcibly converted to Islam. It was a period of total devastation in Kodagu. In order to repopulate his kingdom, Dodda Veerarajendra had to attract people from other parts of the region. After Tipu's treaty with the British in 1792, about 12,000 converted Kodavas in Srirangapatna escaped and came back to their homeland. They eagerly sought reunion with their families. Unfortunately, the conservative Kodavas did not accept them back into their fold. Descendants of these Muslims are still in some parts of Kodagu and are known as Kodava Mapillas. However, Veerarajendra gave them land and in some cases even restored their family properties.

Similarly, Tipu had reportedly transported about 70,000 Christians from Kanara to Srirangapatna and forced Islam on them. By 1792, there were barely 10,000 survivors among them. Out of these about 700 escaped and Veerarajendra invited them to Virajpet to settle down, as they could not go back to Kanara, which was still under Tipu's control. He agreed to build a church for them. By a decree issued on 10 November 1792, the raja of Coorg ordered a church to be constructed and granted land and funds for the purpose. Father Joa D'Costa from Goa was the first vicar of this church, which was named after Saint Anne. Veerarajendra also presented a gold crown, a brass lamp, and an ornamental brass box to the church. The brass lamp is still in use in the church. A more spacious church was built in the year 1811. Again, in 1868, the structure was dismantled and was replaced by a new church in its present Gothic style.

In 1757, after the defeat of Nawab Siraj-ud-Daula by the

British in the Battle of Plassey, a number of Bengali Muslims who feared persecution came down south and settled in Kochi and Kannur. About hundred descendants of these Bengali Muslims from Kannur, in response to Veerarajendra's invitation, came over to the newly founded town of Virajpet during mid-1790s in search of new opportunities. The area where they settled is to this day known as Bengali Street.

The brass lamp donated to the church by Veerarajendra

Over a period of time, Veerarajendra's Virajpet attracted Bunts, Gowdas and Brahmins from South Kanara, Moplas from Malabar, Tamilians from Madras, Gowligas and Telugu Chettis from Andhra, and Devangas and Jains from Mysore areas. Besides Bengali Street, there is a Telugu Street and a Jain Street in Virajpet as well. All these immigrants have made profound contributions in shaping Kodagu as it is today. This diverse population has had a significant impact on the evolution of the Kodava language as well.

After the British takeover of Kodagu in 1834,

Veerarajendrapette came to be known as Virajpet, and was made the Taluk Headquarters. The Virajpet Civil Court was established in 1885.

It was the Mukkatira family that erected the most visible landmark of Virajpet—the clock tower—in 1914, to commemorate the Coronation Durbar of King George V. Since membership to clubs started by the British were strictly for the whites, some of the prominent citizens in and around Virajpet started the Victoria Club in 1887 on a land donated by Chepudira Thimmayya, the grandson of Dewan Chepudira Ponnappa. It still continues to be an active centre for social activities. Virajpet has steadily grown over the centuries and has become an important trading town.

A KINGDOM REGAINED

Whenever he saw his bouncy eight-year-old daughter Rajammaji, Veerarajendra was reminded of that cold December night in 1788 when he and his family escaped from Tipu's clutches in Periapatna. It was a night he would never forget. He felt a sharp tinge of guilt at having nearly lost the infant Rajammaji that night whom he had ordered silenced, lest the guards discover them during their flight. He was ever grateful to Hombale Nayaka and Ismail Khan for helping him and his family in their getaway. Veerarajendra rewarded them handsomely for having saved the life of little Rajammaji. Consequently, Hombale Nayaka was appointed as one of his dewans.

By 1795, Veerarajendra had fully secured Haleri dynasty's realm. His military alliance with the British East India Company had proved to be the most prudent move. It was due to this friendship treaty that his adversary Tipu Sultan was kept at bay, and Kodagu saw unprecedented peace since 1791. For his safety and that of his family, Veerarajendra had identified a suitable spot for the construction of a palace at the remote and not too easily accessible valley in Nalaknad. This piece of land belonged to Pulliyanda okka. He persuaded the head of the Pulliyanda family to surrender the area, and in lieu compensated the displaced family with a larger extent of land in Maggula village. Soon, Veerarajendra moved into his new dwelling in December 1791 where his family was relatively safe. Even though his capital was at Madikeri, he preferred spending time at Nalaknad.

Veerarajendra had made it a tradition to celebrate the harvest festival—Puthari—at Nalaknad. The paddy fields around the palace had a bumper crop that year in 1795. In December that year he decided to make Puthari a grand show. Veerarajendra had captured a large cache of arms and ammunitions from Tipu's four forts established during the Tiger of Mysore's occupation of Kodagu. Amongst them were several cannons supplied by the French to Tipu Sultan. He arranged for twenty-one of these cannons to be mounted near the palace; and as soon as he harvested the first sheaf of paddy at an auspicious time, he ordered his men to fire volleys into the full moon sky. It was a spectacular display never witnessed before in the region. Wild animals and roosting birds shrieked and fled helter-skelter. The entire valley reverberated to the sound of cannon fire. His senior dewans and other officers were invited along with hundreds of villagers from the neighbourhood. Rajammaji preceded her father holding the tray with the lamp as Veerarajendra brought the fresh harvest to the palace, followed by his retinue carrying oil-soaked torches. His royal consort Nanjammaji washed his feet at the palace steps to a crescendo of trumpets and drums. Once inside the palace, Nanjammaji offered her husband the customary silver cup full of warm milk. Later all were treated to a grand feast—thombarada oota—prepared in the palace kitchen. (Hundreds of these cannon balls fired during Puthari festivals are now in the possession of Apparanda family who discovered them while opening up their coffee estate in Nalaknad village.)

Twelve years had passed by since Veerarajendra married

Nanjammaji. She had conducted herself admirably as his royal consort. However, the raja was disappointed that she could not bear him a male heir. He had several sons and daughters by his minor wives but they were not eligible to succeed him to the throne of Kodagu, which he had secured with blood, sweat and tears. He yearned for a son to perpetuate the Haleri dynasty.

Mantap in Nalaknad where the marriage and coronation of Veerarajendra was held in 1796

It was customary for Lingayat rajas to take a royal consort once every twelve years. Veerarajendra invoked this custom, and Nanjammaji faithfully welcomed the decision. Veerarajendra took nearly a year to find a suitable bride for himself. The choice fell on Mahadevammaji, the beautiful sister of one of his treasury officials—Karanika Subbaiah. The thirty-three-year-old Veerarajendra celebrated his formal coronation, and marriage to

Mahadevammaji in February 1796. A specially-built mantap in front of his palace at Nalaknad was the venue for these twin events. It was a grand affair and was attended by some of the British officers sent as representatives of his friend General Sir Robert Abercrombie. The bride and groom were wished many years of happy married life, and his subjects prayed for the royal couple to be soon blessed with a male heir. Thereafter, Mahadevammaji became Veerarajendra's principal wife. After these accomplishments, Veerarajendra added the suffix Wodeyar to his name.

In the meantime, Tipu Sultan had started mobilizing his forces and the British were highly concerned with his growing prowess. The East India Company again sought Veerarajendra's help for the fourth and final battle with Tipu in 1799. Veerarajendra left no stone unturned in making all possible arrangements for the British troops from Bombay under General James Stuart to pass through Kodagu and to engage Tipu's army. A field hospital was set up at Virajpet to treat the wounded. Veerarajendra organized for provisions, bullock-carts, footmen and other logistical support to the British troops. He offered to go along with the British army with his Kodava warriors so that he could avenge the atrocities committed by Tipu on his family and subjects. However, the British declined as they found Kodagu warriors more adept at guerrilla tactics than in regimented warfare in the battle field.

Following the defeat and demise of Tipu in 1799, threats of invasions receded. Veerarajendra settled down to rebuilding his kingdom. The British, led by Colonel Arthur Wellesley (later Duke of Wellington), were most grateful to him for his assistance. The raja received a magnificently crafted sword as a personal gift from Marques Wellesley, the governor general and brother of Arthur Wellesley. Veerarajendra maintained cordial relationship with the British, and the friendship treaty he signed with them insured his kingdom from external threats. However, when the British wanted him to pay them the annual tribute of 24,000 rupees, previously demanded and taken under duress by Hyder Ali and Tipu, he strongly protested. Veerarajendra knew that it was at the instigation of Dewan Purnayya that the British were making this demand. He made a spirited representation to the British governor at Madras not to be swayed by the wily Brahmin, whose long-standing aim was to make Kodagu a part of Mysore. Finally, the British settled for a gift of an elephant every year from the raja of Kodagu.

Veerarajendra encouraged people displaced from Kodagu during Hyder Ali's and Tipu's reigns, to come back and resettle in their ancestral properties. At the same time, he evicted a number of outsiders to whom Tipu had granted land in Kodagu during his occupation.

In the next five years, his favourite wife Mahadevammaji gave birth to two daughters. Veerarajendra hoped to be soon blessed with a son who would carry on his mantle.

Meanwhile, his eldest daughter Rajammaji continued to be the apple of his eye. She had grown into a beautiful young girl and was fast coming of age. He wanted to make amends for the trauma that Rajammaji had to go through as a child, by getting her a groom from another royal lineage. After much searching, an offer was sent in 1797 to Basavalingaraja, a prince from the Sode royal family. The Sode dynasty had been ruling Sirsi in the northern part of Karnataka since 1555. However, their long reign was terminated by Hyder Ali in 1763, and the deposed royal family sought asylum in Goa's territories which was at the time under Portuguese control. The surviving members of the illustrious Sode royalty had lost all their wealth, and were living in near penury in Goa.

Veerarajendra obtained special permission from the Portuguese governor of Goa for the bridegroom, Sode Basavalingaraja, to travel to Kodagu in December 1801. Rajammaji's marriage was celebrated in the same mantap in Nalaknad Palace where Veerarajendra's wedding to Mahadevammaji was held. The festivities lasted for nine days. As a wedding gift, Veerarajendra gave the newlyweds the annual interest of six thousand rupees earned from a deposit of one lakh rupees that he had kept with the East India Company in Bombay. This amount would keep his daughter in good comfort. Sode Raja finally returned to Goa with his bride Rajammaji after spending three months in Kodagu.

In 1805, much to everyone's disappointment, another daughter was born to Mahadevammaji. Veerarajendra gradually turned despondent and was increasingly becoming ill-tempered. He was depressed at not yet having begotten a male heir. He pined for a son, whom he envisioned grooming to be a great king.

Veerarajendra's attempts to lift his spirits with various activities did not help overcome his depression. Then one day, while interacting with some British officers, he expressed his desire to own a lion, and that he wished to be remembered as the 'Lion of Kodagu' to contrast with the sobriquet 'Tiger of Mysore' attributed to his arch enemy Tipu Sultan. He had the royal emblem designed with images of lions on them even though his kingdom abounded with tigers. However, he had never seen a living specimen of a lion. When this news reached Jonathan Duncan, the governor of Bombay at the time, he readily agreed to present a lion to the raja from the fledgling zoo that the British had established there. Veerarajendra sent Jemedhar Monniah and Sankaraiah to Bombay to fetch the animal to Kodagu. The two men had the unenviable task of carting the lion, and after two months of leaving Bombay, they reached Kodagu in the middle of 1805 with the precious cargo. The lion was in good fettle till they reached the banks of river Kavery at Bethari in southern part of Kodagu. While camping at this place and making arrangements to cross the river, there was a heavy monsoon downpour. The beast, not used to wet weather, suddenly took ill. It shivered violently and within hours the lion was dead. With bated breath, the men conveyed the bad news to the raja. Veerarajendra was highly disappointed. As a consolation, he had the animal stuffed and displayed at the Madikeri Fort. He, however, took the demise of the lion as an inauspicious omen.

Veerarajendra was already disturbed by rumours of conspiracies against him, some incriminating even his brothers Appajiraja and Lingarajendra. In what followed, several of his purported enemies were put to death, some of them at his own hands. Veerarajendra lost his robust personality and started looking haggard and aged.

Around this time, his friend and well-wisher, General Abercrombie, who had returned to England, wrote enquiring about his health, and wanted to know about the progress in recording the history of the Haleri dynasty. Veerarajendra finally took on this project, which came as a welcome diversion for the melancholy raja. His narration to the scribes was compiled as *Rajendraname*. This is the only written documentation of the early history of Kodagu, starting with his ancestor Veerappa, who came to the land disguised as a jangama and established the Haleri dynasty in early seventeenth century. General Abercrombie translated *Rajendraname* to English and it was published in 1808.

In December 1805, the raja received some good news to lift his sagging morale. His daughter Rajammaji gave birth to a son at the Madikeri Palace. The child was named Sode Sadashivaraja.

LAST WILL AND TESTAMENT OF VEERARAJENDRA

In January 1807, Mahadevammaji was in labour to deliver her fourth child. There were hectic activities in Madikeri Palace as midwives scurried around in the queen's chambers. Veerarajendra paced anxiously in the corridor. His beloved rani was not in the best of health, and this was in all probability the last child she would bear. Raja's astrologers had nervously predicted the birth of a son to please him. They sat in the anteroom and were more anxious than anyone else. If this child also turned out to be a female, they would in all certainly lose their heads.

Late in the evening, Veerarajendra heard Mahadevammaji's painful shrieks. A little later, the child announced its arrival with a squeal. The king waited for the maidservant to rush to him with the news. There was a delay. He turned apprehensive. The newborn continued to yell but the servants were terrified of breaking the news of the arrival of yet another girl child to the raja. Finally, Veerarajendra himself barged into Mahadevammaji's room. When he was received by sombre faces, he knew that there was no son born to continue his legacy. Mahadevammaji was exhausted after the accouchement. He then heard the feeble voice of his wife, 'Forgive me, Mahaswami.'

The raja was sad, furious and despondent. Unable to control his anger, he shouted his instructions to the African Siddi guards.

They hurried towards the room where the three astrologers sat waiting for what was in store for them. If the newborn was a male, they would be showered with gold coins and grant of land. Otherwise, it could be death. When they saw the dreaded Siddis, they knew their fate.

Meanwhile, Mahadevammaji faded with each passing day. Veerarajendra tried all he could to save his beloved wife. On a gloomy Sunday, 17 May 1807, Veerarajendra watched Mahadevammaji helplessly as she breathed her last. Heartbroken, he went into deep depression. He could not come to terms with the loss of his favourite wife and companion. He felt desolate and started fearing for the life of his four young daughters, now left without a mother. The eldest of the daughters, Devammaji, was eight years old. He suspected that the cause of ill-health and death of Mahadevammaji was slow poisoning. Even his other wives and their children were not beyond his suspicion. In order to personally guard their safety, he kept the four girls close to his dwelling.

However, his worst fear was what his two brothers—Appajiraja and Lingarajendra—would do after his passing. He was certain that they would usurp the throne and put all his children to the sword. He hated the conceited Appajiraja and the uncouth Lingarajendra. Slowly but surely, Veerarajendra was turning paranoid. He grew more and more distrustful of his close aides. If he suspected anyone in his court, he would have the person beheaded or thrown in jail. A few of his trusted supporters were shot dead by the raja himself. His ardent supporters, who were devoted to him, now found it very difficult to function in his court.

By the end of 1807, the raja's mental condition had

deteriorated to such an extent that some of the Kodava leaders along with the palace guards hatched a plot to assassinate the paranoiac Veerarajendra. But, one of the spies whispered about the plot to him. The conspirators planned to storm his private chambers in the night and slay the raja. Veerarajendra gave instructions to his Siddi bodyguards to lay in wait and close all the gates leading to the fort as soon as the traitors came inside. Late in the night, about three hundred men entered the fort armed with swords and spears. Before they sneaked into the palace where Veerarajendra lived, the king emulated a scheme used by his bête noire Hyder Ali. He hid in a safe place and kept a bundle of clothes on his four-poster bed to make it appear as though he was sleeping under the blanket. A handful of the assassins slipped into his chambers and cut the form inside the blanket to pieces. They immediately realized that they were trapped. As they ran out to the yard where the rest of the men waited, Veerarajendra ordered his bodyguards to massacre all the conspirators. The rebels had no way of escaping from the fort. Veerarajendra stood at the balcony and fired at the plotters, killing twenty-five of them. The bloodthirsty Siddis cut down almost all the nearly 300 intruders. The courtyard was filled with ankle-deep blood as it overflowed onto the streets outside. The following day, several of the suspected senior officials in his court were summarily executed, and in some cases entire families were exterminated.

Veerarajendra was obsessed with ways to ensure that he was succeeded by one of his own progeny. Not having a son to inherit his legacy was corroding his psyche. His first choice was the eldest daughter Devammaji born to Mahadevammaji. The only hope he had of ensuring succession of his descendants to the throne of Kodagu was to have his will and testament registered with the British. Veerarajendra wrote a letter to the British Governor General Lord Minto on 7 October 1807, giving details of his succession. In his elaborate will, he requested the British to ensure that his nine-year-old daughter Devammaji be made queen after his demise. He named his son-in-law Sode Basavalingaraja the regent till Devammaji and her husband were old enough to take control of the domain. He wanted the male child of Devammaji to be named 'Veerarajendra' and to be anointed as the next king of Kodagu. He bequeathed his ring with the royal insignia, and the sword presented by Governor General Marques Wellesley to the yet to be born grandson. The will also detailed that should Devammaji not have a male heir, then the son born to her sisters depending on their seniority should be the successor. If none of the four daughters had a male child, then the fittest amongst his three sons (Rajashekara, Shashishankara and Chandrashekara) born to his minor wives was to ascend to the throne of Kodagu.

In 1808, Devammaji was barely nine years old when he arranged her marriage to Mallappa, a young Kodava, who was earlier converted to the Lingayat sect. The raja lived in dread of spells and incantations being cast on him and his family by his enemies. One morning he got up from bed startled as a result of dreadful nightmares. On an impulse, he summoned his Siddi guards and ordered them to bring him the heads of his brothers Appajiraja and Lingarajendra. Appajiraja lived close to Madikeri at Appangala. The ruthless Siddis found Appajiraja basking in the morning sun. They fell on him and severed his head as his wife and children watched in horror.

After ordering the assassination of his brothers,

Veerarajendra sat all by himself in his room and suddenly felt terrible remorse at his rash decision. He called his soldiers and instructed them to go after the Siddis to stop the murders. The angels of mercy were too late for Appajiraja, but they managed to stop the group of assassins headed to faraway Haleri where Lingarajendra lived. Veerarajendra spent the next few days in utter misery. On being summoned a trembling Lingarajendra came to his brother, lay prostrate in front of him, and swore, 'Mahaswami, I will always remain your faithful servant.' Veerarjendra's life was in total disarray. He wept, and had elaborate shanti poojas performed to atone for his sins.

In January 1809, Arthur Cole, the British resident at Mysore, received news of Veerarajendra's mental health and rumours of his atrocities. The raja alternated between dejection and fits of rage. Arthur Cole sent his physician Dr Ingledew to Coorg to treat the raja. Dr Ingledew's medicines and counselling put Veerarajendra at ease. He felt relatively safe for the first time after the demise of Mahadevammaji. However, Veerarajendra feared that Dr Ingledew would come to know of the details of all the massacres, and that this would be communicated to the governor general in Calcutta. Veerarajendra did not want the British to take a dim view of him, and consequently disregard his will.

Veerarajendra showed signs of improvement and the doctor returned to Mysore. But, within days, Veerarajendra drifted back to his miserable frame of mind. His suspicion of people around him started to haunt him once more. In February that year, on his instructions, the Siddi executioners decapitated four of his senior kariakaras and dewans. The following day, he had a total memory lapse and asked for the slain principal officers. When told that they had been executed in accordance with his orders, Veerarajendra relapsed into severe depression. He bit his hand in despair and the deep gash started bleeding profusely. As he staggered up the stairs, he stumbled and fell. The fall dislocated his arm. In spite of intense pain, he locked himself in his room for several days, refusing food and medicine.

Dr Ingledew came to Madikeri to treat the raja. Veerarajendra expressed his deepest regret at the death of his principal officers, which he attributed to his momentary insanity. He incredulously charged his subordinates and put the onus on them for their slavish actions! In an act to impress the British doctor, Veerarajendra attempted suicide by cutting his own throat. Dr Ingledew rushed to his chambers to discover the cut not to be life threatening. On the suggestion of the doctor, the British Resident Arthur Cole made a trip to Mercara to meet the raja. Arthur Cole assured the raja that the British recognized his assistance to them and would continue to be friends of the raja in accordance with the treaty signed in 1791. Arthur Cole promised that he would strongly recommend to the governor general and that the British would honour the raja's will and testament. Subsequently, in April 1809, a letter arrived from the Governor General Lord Minto, officially recognizing the will. The British agreed to be guardians to his children. This news finally calmed the nerves of Veerarajendra.

It was around this time that the writing of *Rajendraname*, the historical account of the Haleri kings, was completed. Veerarajendra attached his 'Last Will and Testament' at the end of this manuscript.

Veerarajendra deposited an equivalent of 5,40,000 rupees in the treasury of the East India Company at Madras. In his will he directed that, out of this sum, bonds for one lakh of rupees each should be taken in the names of his grandsons Sode Sadashivaraja and the yet-to-be-born 'Veerarajendra'. The remaining three lakh forty thousand were to be in the name of his daughter Devammaji who would be the queen. Subsequently, a further amount equivalent to three lakh rupees was deposited in the Bombay branch of East India Company in Devammaji's name. Earlier, he had deposited one lakh of rupees in the British treasury in favour of his eldest daughter Rajammaji who was married to Sode Basavalingaraja. In addition, he had an investment of two lakh rupees with the East India Company for the benefit of his other children.

After the issue of succession was placed in the hands of the British, whom he trusted more than anyone else, Veerarajendra had a brief spell of respite from the demons that were troubling him. Sadly, his peace of mind was soon disturbed as memories of his role in killing hundreds of his close family members and some of his devoted subjects came to trouble him again. Every place he went to reminded him of the blood he had spilled. He was in constant terror of the ghosts of the dead haunting him. He lapsed into yet another bout of misanthropy. His subjects dreaded him lest he suddenly explode in a fit of rage and inflict horrendous punishments. With his condition deteriorating, Dr Ingledew was once again summoned to Mercara to treat the raja. By then, he was far too gone and was on his deathbed. On 9 June 1809, he called for his daughter Devammaji to his bedside. He handed the ten-year-old heir-apparent his ring with the royal seal. Shortly afterwards, Veerarajendra died holding the hands of his daughters Devammaji and Rajammaji. He was aged forty-six. It was a sad and gloomy end of a king who was the

Royal tombs at Gaddige, Madikeri

hero in the history of Kodagu. In accordance with his wishes, he was buried next to his beloved consort Mahadevammaji, at the royal tombs in Gaddige near Madikeri.

LINGARAJENDRA THE LUCKY

Lingarajendra, the youngest brother of Veerarajendra, was given the jagir at Haleri. He lived a quiet life in the old palace, surrounded by thick forest, where his ancestors had first established their foothold in Kodagu. Lingarajendra enjoyed cultivating his land. Besides, the environment was ideal for pursuing his passion—hunting. The wooded area provided bountiful wild game. Lingarajendra was a crack-shot, an able archer and proficient at wielding weapons like odikathi, the Kodava knife, and the spear. His favourite hunting technique was to impale a wild boar while on horseback. He could shoot a moving target while riding his horse.

On a bright morning in February 1808, he was busy preparing for a hunting expedition. His young assistant, the lame Basava, whom Lingarajendra called Kunta Basava, was helping him with getting all the weapons and the dogs ready. His six-year-old son Chikka Veerarajendra was busy playing with a wooden toy gun.

The large pack of his hunting dogs suddenly started barking, and he knew that someone was approaching his property. A little later, he heard voices and sound of horses galloping towards his palace. With a sense of foreboding, he awaited the visitors. He first saw a posse of Siddi bodyguards of the raja. He froze at the sight of these dreaded assassins. The news of the massacre at Madikeri Fort a few months ago was fresh in his memory. As the Africans advanced, immediately behind them on two horses, rode regular soldiers. They overtook the Siddis and stopped them from moving forward. On the directives of Veerarajendra, the Siddis were on a mission to take Lingarajendra's head as a trophy to the raja. As luck would have it, Veerarajendra had reversed his impulsive orders, and had sent the soldiers to stop the execution. Lingarajendra was saved minutes before he was to be beheaded.

The soldiers confided in Lingarajendra the increasing fits of rage and suspicion that Veerarajendra displayed since the death of his favourite consort Mahadevammaji. They advised him to pay a visit to the raja and assure him of his loyalty since he was extremely unhappy about not having a male heir to succeed him on the throne of Kodagu.

The following day, Lingarajendra hastened to Madikeri, deliberately dressed as a humble farmer. He fell at his brother's feet and declared his everlasting allegiance to him and his family. Lingarajendra was conscious of Veerarajendra's dislike of him, and took care not to antagonize the unstable raja. He was surprised when Veerarajendra came and hugged him and started sobbing on his shoulders. The king was highly repentant of his atrocious actions, which had cost the life of their brother Appajiraja. The raja further amazed him when he announced that Lingarajendra would inherit Appajiraja's property, and bestowed him with the guardianship of the slain brother's family.

Lingarajendra's astute eyes did not fail to notice the angst-ridden expressions on the faces of those present at the court. Veerarajendra was losing the devotion and loyalty that he had commanded earlier from his subjects. Lingarajendra, however, was aware of the elaborate course of action that Veerarajendra had worked out with the British, regarding succession after his demise. He saw a glimmer of opportunity for himself in the fragile environment at Madikeri. While showing absolute subservience to his imposing brother, he now secretly entertained the idea of a possibility of capturing the throne of Kodagu.

After Veerarajendra's gloomy end on 9 June 1809, physician Dr Ingledew was deputed as the British representative by Arthur Cole to oversee the smooth transfer of power. Dr Ingledew had many sessions of discussions with the Kodava panchayat and with their consent, he decided to honour the will of the late raja. In accordance with the will, Sode Basavalingaraja assumed control of administration as the principal dewan with the ten-year-old Devammaji anointed as the queen. The people of Kodagu silently welcomed the demise of the demented Veerarajendra. They now looked forward to peace and stability in the kingdom, unmindful of who sat on the throne.

Lingarajendra did not remain inactive for long. Within weeks, he started his intrigues and spread discontent amongst the Kodavas for being ruled by a foreigner from faraway Goa. He predicted that one day the foreigner would usurp the throne for himself.

He argued and pleaded that he, being Devammaji's uncle, should be the regent to the young queen in place of Sode Raja. Aware of the hold the British had on the kingdom, he ingratiated himself with Dr Ingledew and gained his sympathy. Another meeting of the Kodava panchayat was convened at Madikeri. After deliberating for hours, the majority of Kodava elders rejected Lingarajendra's proposition and decided to adhere to the will left by Veerarajendra.

Lingarajendra was utterly disappointed and dejected.

Crestfallen, he trotted on horseback out of Mercara Fort towards Haleri with tears rolling down his cheeks. His faithful servant, Kunta Basava, was the only one to accompany him. Luckily, on his way he met one of the highly respected and influential dewans, Chowrira Appanna, who was late for the assembly of elders. Dewan Appanna, who knew Lingarajendra since childhood, was sorry to see him in such a miserable state. Lingarajendra poured his heart out to the dewan and narrated the adverse turn of events. Again, Lady Luck smiled on Lingarajendra. Dewan Appanna got swayed by Lingarajendra's plea and promised to help him secure the regency of Kodagu. He took him back to the Kodava panchayat and forcefully argued his case. Appanna challenged his colleagues to respond to his contention: 'Why should we kowtow to a person who does not belong to the Haleri dynasty when we have a scion of the family, Lingarajendra, with us?' These arguments made the congregation reconsider their decision. Lingarajendra was amazed when the Kodava panchayat, after brief deliberations, changed their earlier stand and preferred him as regent instead of the raja of Sode.

Dr Ingledew was overtaken by these fast-changing events. He was, however, not in favour of replacing Sode Basavalingaraja without consulting the governor general at Calcutta. In the meantime, the immature and frightened Rani Devammaji petitioned Dr Ingledew that she would like her uncle Lingarajendra to guide her and be her Lord Protector. These developments in Madikeri unnerved Sode Raja. With the people of Kodagu rallying behind Lingarajendra, he feared for his own safety. Basavalingaraja requested Dr Ingledew to relieve him of his responsibilities, and made an appeal for grant of one lakh of rupees and another four thousand rupees towards his travel expenses back to his hometown Bandewadi in Goa. Lingarajendra who had already assumed the role of regent, readily agreed to settle this amount, and have the Sode Raja and his family exit Kodagu as early as possible. The British too gave their nod and Basavalingaraja was given these funds from the treasury of Kodagu. By December 1809, he left Kodagu along with his wife Rajammaji and their infant son Sadashivaraja.

Lingarajendra did not waste time in taking complete control of the administration of Kodagu. Thereafter, he set himself on gaining total support of the British. He deputed three of his senior officials namely Chepudira Ponnappa, Parsee Hirjee and Muthanna to Madras with gifts for the Governor Sir George Barlow. Lingarajendra also sent a letter emphasising his allegiance to the British. In the meantime, Dr Ingledew had already sent a report to the governor endorsing the sincerity of Lingarajendra.

Lingarajendra's delegation promptly brought back a letter of thanks from the governor, appreciating his efforts in ushering peace in his kingdom, and for taking on the responsibility of looking after the young Rani Devammaji and the other children of his late brother Veerarajendra.

Within a year, Lingarajendra completely mesmerized the innocent Rani Devammaji to concede the throne in his favour. Under his overbearing persuasion, Devammaji affixed her signature to a letter written on 9 September 1810, addressed to the British governor in Madras, relinquishing 'of her own free will' the throne of Kodagu to her thirty-four-year-old uncle. Even though the British governor in Madras, Sir Barlow, and the Governor General Lord Hastings in Calcutta did not find these developments in accordance with Veerarajendra's will, they glossed over Lingarajendra's cunning schemes. Lingarajendra, who was perceived as rather dull and harmless, surprised the people of Kodagu when he declared himself the raja in 1811. He immediately named his only son, the eight-year-old Chikka Veerarajendra, as his heir-apparent.

Once firmly on the throne of Kodagu, Lingarajendra set his eyes on the large amounts of funds invested by his brother Dodda Veerarajendra with the East India Company at Madras and Bombay in his daughter Devammaji's name, and for the comforts of his other children. He persuaded the British to have the amount and the interest dues transferred in his favour. The British finally agreed to pay the annual interest to Lingarajendra, which they wanted to be used for the benefit of ex-Rani Devammaji and her sisters. By now, the British had effectively disregarded the will of the elder Veerarajendra. Lingarajendra was, however, apprehensive of the British and he took great care to keep them well-humoured lest they changed their mind. He also ensured that none of his subjects leaked news of his administration to the British. Suspected informants were dealt with severely. He virtually sealed the borders of Kodagu and did not permit any of his citizens to leave the country.

In the next few years, having successfully secured his position, Lingarajendra turned highly autocratic, suspicious and vindictive. Dewan Appanna, the man responsible for Lingarajendra's ascendancy to the throne of Kodagu, bitterly regretted his actions. Lingarajendra had grown-up in the midst of lowly servants, and even after his elevation to the throne, he was more comfortable in the company of charlatans and sycophants. Kunta Basava, who was Lingarajendra's dog-keeper at Haleri, started asserting himself as his master's henchman. Lingarajendra did not relish the advice of learned elders at court who counselled him to show restraint and shun his tyrannical attitude. Dewan Appanna was forthright in his criticism of Lingarajendra's conduct. A peeved Lingarajendra charged the elderly dewan with treason. Accusing Appanna as a desadrohi, Lingarajendra himself carried out the investigation.

Under tremendous pressure, the elderly dewan was forced to 'confess' his guilt. However, an unrelenting Dewan Appanna's admission was: 'I am guilty indeed, of one crime, of having made a wretch like you the raja of Kodagu.' Enraged, Lingarajendra had the dewan tied to a tree and shot with arrows.

The ill-tempered Lingarajendra is known to have been extremely harsh on his subjects. He was notorious for summary executions. It is reported that during his reign, he personally killed at least 2,500 of his citizens. Once, loud trumpeting by two of his elephants in Madikeri Fort disturbed his sleep. In a fit of rage, Lingarajendra carried his gun and shot down the elephants. The next morning he repented his impulsive actions. The two behemoths were well-trained and were his favourite animals. He used to ride them as mahout during his frequent shikars. In their memory, he had two life-size statues of the elephants installed, which are still in the Madikeri Fort premises.

Lingarajendra had another sadistic way of inflicting capital punishment on those awarded the death penalty. The doomed 'culprits' (about half a dozen at a time) would be made to run in front of the courtyard of the palace towards the exit gate of the fort. This measured about 200 metres. Lingarajendra, sitting at the balcony along with his heir-apparent, would shoot down the hapless prisoners as they ran for their lives. If anyone dodged the bullets and ran out of the gate, his life would be spared. However, it is reported that only a handful escaped Lingarajendra's deadly aim.

Lingarajendra was fortunate not to have any skirmishes during his reign, and the general population lived in relative peace. He encouraged agriculture and laid down detailed instructions for revenue collection. Land tax was assessed not on the extent of land, but on the fertility of the soil. One of Lingarajendra's prized crops was cardamom, which he purchased from his subjects and kept the stock stored in built-in bins under his cot. He frequently exchanged this spice for fine Arabian horses from the traders of Kerala.

He was shrewd enough to keep the British happy, and diligently sustained the friendship treaty that his brother had signed with the East India Company. He also took good care of the family of Dodda Veerarajendra and Appajiraja and continued the practice of sending an elephant every year as a gift to the British. Lingarajendra is known for arranging spectacular hunting expeditions for his European guests. One of his fetishes was to dress in the uniform of a British major general, and his heir-apparent in that of a general while meeting the British. Lingarajendra died in 1820. His son Chikka Veerarajendra, the last king of Kodagu, succeeded him after his death.

STORY OF THATHANDA SUBBAYYA

Lingarajendra had reasons to be in high spirits. He had not only successfully secured the throne of Kodagu for himself but also maneuvered the British East India Company to support his clever machinations. No wonder he was savouring every moment at his darbar in Madikeri Fort. His son and heir-apparent Chikka Veerarajendra was seated next to him. His trusted lieutenant Kunta Basava occupied a prominent place in the court as the newly promoted jamedar. The raja and his entourage had just been entertained by a group of dancing girls.

It was March 1811. The weather was fine and the revenue collection had been good. His people had leisure till the onset of the monsoon in June. For Lingarajendra, it was the ideal time to indulge in his favourite pastime—shikar. Lingarajendra was keen on taking his eight-year-old yuvaraja on a hunting expedition. Just as Lingarajendra broached the topic of the shikar, a messenger came and handed him a letter from Arthur Cole, the British resident at Mysore, who also served as ex-officio resident of Coorg. He opened the letter with trepidation. Lately, Lingarajendra's greatest preoccupation had been to not in any way upset the British, lest they change their minds and support his brother's minor daughter Devammaji in accordance with the will of Dodda Veerarajendra. To his relief, the contents of the letter spelled out to be a wonderful opportunity to please the white man. The letter was an introduction to Colonel James

Welsh (later general) and his assistant, Lieutenant Williamson. Both the officers were keen on hunting, and having heard about the abundance of wild game in Kodagu, wanted a shikar organized for them.

Lingarajendra shown engaged in hunting in a drawing by Thippajappa of Shimoga

Lingarajendra immediately instructed his aides to make all the arrangements for the hunt and overnight camping in the forest. He got the guest house near the fort at Madikeri, built during Dodda Veerarajendra's reign, spruced up and ready for the British visitors. A cook, well-versed in preparing European dishes, was told to stock provisions necessary to cater to the needs of the guests. Lingarajendra deputed one of his able army commanders and an excellent shikari, Kariakara Thathanda Subbayya, to oversee the arrangements for the hunt.

The two British officers were the first representatives of the East India Company to visit Kodagu after Lingarajendra's ascent to the throne. Lingarajendra was anxious to leave an indelible impression on his guests. When Colonel Welsh and Lieutenant Williamson reached Madikeri in palanquins provided by Lingarajendra, they were surprised to see the raja himself at the entrance to the palace ready to welcome them. They were amused to see Lingarajendra in a British major general's uniform, and his nine-year-old son, and heir-apparent, in a general's uniform!

The following morning, Lingarajendra astonished his guests once again by arriving at the guesthouse to personally take them on the hunt. He had brought elephants, horses and a retinue of servants with a whole range of weapons, all ready for the shikar. He told his guests that a wild elephant was on a rampage in a village close by and he wanted to destroy the beast. Both the British officers were excited at the opportunity of witnessing such a spectacular event. Lingarajendra sat on the neck of one of his well-trained elephants substituting for the mahout. The colonel and his assistant sat on the back of the same elephant. Thathanda Subbayya was already in the forest along with an advance party of hunters. On a cue from the raja, the forest reverberated to the sound of hundreds of drums. The rogue elephant was chased towards where Lingarajendra and his visitors sat on machaans (platforms) built on treetops. Lingarajendra had already explained to his guests that the only way to bring down an elephant was to shoot it in the temple. The terrified elephant charged towards the trees where the raja and his guests sat. As it approached the tree where Williamson sat, the lieutenant shot the beast as instructed by the raja. The elephant fell to the ground trumpeting in agony, its bulk breaking branches of small trees and smothering the undergrowth. Soon there was silence that was broken by loud cheering from the hunters as the raja and his guest came down to see the fallen animal. It was a magnificent specimen and had huge tusks measuring three feet in length. Williamson was awestruck at the trophy he had bagged. Subbayya had arranged a hearty lunch in the middle of the forest in a makeshift hut which had tables and chairs and all the luxuries one could expect in the jungle. The menu included roasted wild boar, pulao and mildly spiced curries. It was an experience that the colonel and his assistant would never forget.

Subbayya's arrangements were marked with clockwork precision and great attention to detail. The raja and his guests were highly impressed and lauded Subbayya's efforts. Colonel Welsh was so impressed that he planned a second visit to Kodagu during October the same year for another hunting expedition.

Lingarajendra summoned Kariakara Subbayya to his court the very next day after his guests departed. Subbayya had played a critical role in pleasing the British. Both Colonel Welsh and Lieutenant Williamson carried unforgettable memories of their visit, and Lingarajendra was aware that they would convey this to their superior officers. In an open court, the raja praised Subbayya for his yeoman service and presented him with a gold bracelet, a gun and a sachet full of gold coins. In addition, Lingarajendra gifted him a painting of himself with Kariakara Thathanda Subbayya standing respectfully paying obeisance to the raja. This painting was framed in ivory with 'Li' inscribed in Kannada. To be included in a painting along with the raja was considered to be one of the greatest felicitation any subject could receive from the king. An emotional Subbayya genuflected and swore unflinching loyalty to his Mahaswami Lingarajendra.

Painting of Thatbanda Subbayya with Lingarajendra (1811)

Kariakara Subbayya's elevation as a favourite of the king caused a great deal of envy amongst the senior officials in the court. They knew that it would only be a matter of time for Subbayya to be promoted as a sarva kariakara. And another couple of years hence he would occupy the coveted position of a dewan. These disgruntled men patiently waited for an opportunity to discredit Subbayya in the eyes of the raja.

Such an occasion presented itself within six months of the visit of the British officers. The farmers from Horoor village made a representation to the raja to eliminate a tiger, which had been lifting their cattle and other livestock. Lingarajendra assured help to the villagers and instructed the kariakaras present in the court to fix a date and organize the hunt. The following day, the kariakaras came to the raja with the suggestion that since Thathanda Subbayya was an expert in constructing machaans and in organizing other activities in the forest, the Mahaswami should entrust Subbayya with this task. Lingarajendra agreed, and Thathanda Subbayya was given the green signal.

Subbayya was only too happy to undertake this task. In earlier years, kariakaras could display their valour in the battlefield but now with no frequent wars, it was on one of these dangerous hunts that they could demonstrate their courage and impress the raja. Subbayya built a machaan using bamboo and cane. He used strong ropes to secure the machaan. It had to be a firm platform that would not shake. A loose machaan could be dangerous as it could make creaking sounds and alert the prey. Even more crucially, it could affect the accuracy of the gunshot. After Subbayya was satisfied with the arrangements, he came to Madikeri to inform Lingarajendra that the hunt could take place the following night. Meanwhile, the tiger remained active in the vicinity of Horoor village.

Subbayya's adversaries, however, had made their plans to sabotage the arrangements. They secretly sent their men to partly cut the ropes used to fasten the machaan.

At the appointed time, Lingarajendra and his team arrived and climbed the tree to sit in wait for the tiger. It was a full moon night and the raja was prepared for a long wait. His guns were loaded and ready. Live bait for the tiger was also tied nearby. A little before midnight, the tiger made its appearance. Lingarajendra knelt and shot the tiger dead with a single shot. With the recoil of the powerful gun, the weakened machaan gave way. It lurched and Lingarajendra was about to fall down from the treetop. But Lingarajendra's agility saved him as he clung to a branch and managed to climb down using the rope ladder. The raja was furious. He thundered, 'Who built this machaan? Bring the rascal immediately, and I will chop his head off myself!'

Subbayya's enemies sidled up to Lingarajendra and complained, 'Mahaswami, ever since you praised him, Subbayya has become very arrogant. Instead of preparing the machaan himself, he delegated the job to his servants.'

At the time of this incident, Subbayya was on another

Tomb of Thathanda Subbayya

treetop, a little away from Lingarajendra. As soon as he heard the gunshot, he came down and started walking towards Lingarajendra and the rest of the hunting party. By then, some of the soldiers were on their way to fetch Subbayya as instructed by the raja. When they met halfway, the soldiers informed Subbayya, 'The raja is furious, and wants to see you immediately.' They then related the episode that had nearly killed Lingarajendra. Lingarajendra's vicious temperament was well-known among his subjects. Subbayya was certain that Lingarajendra would kill him in the most brutal fashion. It did not take him long to infer that this accident was stage managed by his enemies, but the tricky question was: 'How was he to convince the raja?'

Subbayya instructed the soldiers to move on and that he would follow them. He sat down under a huge tree in the middle of the forest. He pointed the barrel of the very gun presented to him by Lingarajendra to his chest. He said a silent prayer to his guru karanas and using his toe pulled the trigger. When the soldiers heard the report, they rushed back only to find Subbayya lying in a pool of blood. They carried Subbayya's body to Lingarajendra and explained the chain of events leading to his death. Lingarajendra was most upset. He had lost his temper, but had no intentions of harming Subbayya in whom he had the greatest of faith. He bitterly mourned the loss of one of his most trusted and efficient army commanders. He vowed to punish the guilty.

Lingarajendra ordered the building of an ornate tomb in memory of Subbayya in his village Kukloor near Virajpet. Subbayya was a bachelor. He had planned on building a house in Kukloor before taking a wife and starting a family. Subbayya's brother Thathanda Poovanna was summoned to the palace and the family was granted land and funds to cultivate paddy. The painting of Lingarajendra with Subbayya bowing to the raja remains a prized possession of the Thathanda family.

THE OMKARESHWARA TEMPLE

After seven years on the throne of Kodagu, Lingarajendra was intoxicated with power and lust. He demanded utmost subservience from his subjects. The slightest suspicion would cost a man his life, and sometimes that of his family as well. At the same time, he himself was constantly in fear of the British East India Company upsetting his position in Kodagu. In order to prevent any news from being transmitted to the British, he employed a network of spies to watch over his subjects. Lingarajendra made it impossible for his people to cross the border of Kodagu. He also wanted to ensure a smooth transfer of power to his son Chikka Veerarajendra, after his demise. In reality, he had no cause to worry about the British since they regarded him as a benign ruler. Nevertheless, Lingarajendra took all measures to keep the officers of the East India Company happy. English visitors to Kodagu were well entertained, and he arranged spectacular shikars for them and bestowed costly gifts on his visitors. According to an Englishman who visited Kodagu during his reign, the raja used to shoot as many tigers as days in a year! Lingarajendra had a veritable zoo in Madikeri fort with exotic animals. His favourite entertainment was to regale his guests with fights between various species of animals. One of his British guests was witness to a fight between a tiger and a bear.

Due to his distrust of others, and fear of conspiracies

against him, Lingarajendra relied on men who were absolutely loyal to him. This resulted in him surrounding himself with sycophants and people of low intellectual calibre. Many of the senior dewans and kariakaras who served his brother Veerarajendra were sidelined. However, as there were no wars during Lingarajendra's reign, the citizens were free to cultivate their lands, and enjoyed peace.

Lingarajendra was also concupiscent and had hundreds of women in his harem. He was notorious for getting good looking young women forcibly converted to the Lingayat sect and taking them as a wife or a concubine. His loyal assistant Kunta Basava aided and abetted the raja in all his wicked activities.

The Haleri dynasty of Lingayat rajas, by tradition, belonged to the priestly class. They rarely needed Brahmins to conduct poojas and other rituals. Because of this, the few Brahmins who lived in Kodagu did not have much importance in the court of the Haleri Kings.

In the year 1817, a poor old Havyak Brahmin from the vicinity of Puttur in Kanara came to Kodagu on foot along with his beautiful young daughter. As the exhausted duo walked up the hill range near Madikeri, a resident of the town, Subarasaiah, encountered them. Subarasaiah, himself a Havyak Brahmin, immediately identified the old man and the young woman as being of the same sect from the way they were dressed, and the fashion in which they wore the sandal paste on their foreheads. Curious, he questioned the old man on the purpose of his visit. The distraught Brahmin confided in Subarasaiah that he was unable to look after his motherless daughter, and that he wanted to meet the Raja of Kodagu and request him to take the young girl as a wife in the harem. He believed his daughter would be well-provided in the palace. An alarmed Subarasaiah took the old man and his daughter to his house and gave them food and shelter for a couple of days. He strongly advised the old Brahmin against his imprudent plans for his young daughter. Luckily, Lingarajendra was away on one of his hunting expeditions at the time. Before the raja's return to Madikeri, Subarasaiah handed over some money and ensured that the old man and his daughter returned to Puttur.

A couple of days later when Lingarajendra got back to his capital, one of his spies informed him about the incident. Lingarajendra was furious at Subarasaiah for thwarting the addition of another beautiful young woman to his harem. He sent his infamous Siddi soldiers to bring Subarasaiah before him. As soon as Subarasaiah saw the Siddis, he knew that his life was in danger. He instructed his shocked wife and children to be prepared to perform his last rites.

'How dare you send away the Brahmin who voluntarily brought his daughter for me?' Lingarajendra bellowed at Subarasaiah. He wanted Subarasaiah to immediately bring back the old man and his daughter. But Subarasaiah confessed that he did what was morally just and that he was not in a position to get the girl back. This enraged Lingarajendra further. He threatened to kill him and his family.

Subarasaiah stood his ground and said, 'The Brahmin and his daughter were strangers, and I have no knowledge of their whereabouts.' This infuriated the raja even more and he ordered the two sons of Subarasaiah to be brought to the fort. He threatened to behead them in front of him if Subarasaiah did not get the young Brahmin woman back to Madikeri. When

Subarasaiah did not relent, he ordered his soldiers to behead the two boys. His command was immediately carried out. A shocked and heartbroken Subarasaiah cursed Lingarajendra and refused to do his bidding.

'I will not let you live in peace. I curse you and your family. May eternal misfortune befall your vamsha,' said Subarasaiah. Lingarajendra was enraged. He ordered the Siddis to cut Subarasaiah limb by limb. As his life ebbed, Subarasaiah kept staring at Lingarajendra, and this image stuck in the mind of the raja.

That night while sleeping, Lingarajendra suddenly woke up and saw Subarasaiah standing in front of his cot. He shouted in horror and called for his bodyguards. His soldiers, however, found no one in the room. After they left, Lingarajendra again saw a ghostly red-eyed Subarasaiah staring at him with the index finger pointed at him. Lingarajendra was totally unnerved. This visit of the apparition continued every night. Some nights he used to wake up with a start and find himself on the floor. Strange things kept happening. This phenomenon recurred almost every night and the raja could not sleep. The image of Subarasaiah's haunting stare totally upset his mental peace. This went on for a month after which Lingarajendra's health deteriorated as a result of sleep deprivation and he could not focus on his regular duties as a raja.

To get rid of this mental trauma, he consulted his astrologers and exorcists but all their mantras and poojas failed to exorcise Subarasaiah's spirit from roaming the palace and tormenting Lingarajendra. It was one of his trusted lieutenants, Karanika Subbaiah, who suggested tantris be invited from Neeleshwar near Mangalore. Karanika Subbaiah was himself entrusted with the task of fetching these famed exorcists to treat the raja.

Soon, the tantris from Neeleshwar were brought to Madikeri as honoured guests of the raja. They made elaborate study of the situation and concluded that the murdered Brahmin Subarasaiah had turned into a Brahma-Rakshasa. The only way to appease his ghost was to build an Eshwara temple at the site near his house and install a Shiva-linga from the holy city of Kashi (Benares). It was also suggested that a suitable grove be provided for the Brahma-Rakshasa to reside and roam within the confines of the temple complex.

Lingarajendra immediately ordered the construction of a temple next to Subarasaiah's house, which was marked according to vastu by the tantris from Neeleshwar. The temple was designed in Islamic style of architecture with a dome in the centre and turrets at the four corners of the square structure. A pond was built in front of the temple with a small mantap in the middle. The entire construction was completed in two years and nine months. A small grove was established at one corner of the temple complex for the spirit of Subarasaiah to reside.

After the construction of the temple, Lingarajendra despatched three well-known Brahmins of Madikeri to bring a Shiva-linga from Kashi. The three men along with some helpers made the long journey to Benares and procured a Shiva-linga, which they manually carried back to Madikeri.

The Shiva-linga was never placed on the ground throughout their two months journey. The Brahmins diligently observed all the rituals while performing daily pooja to the Shiva-linga during the travel.

Omkareshwara Temple

Neeleshwar tantris were once again invited to Madikeri for the installation of the Shiva-linga in the sanctum sanctorum of the newly constructed temple. The Shiva-linga was consecrated on the 26 March 1820. The temple was dedicated to Omkareshwara and the celebrations continued for three days. During this period, feasts were arranged for all the people of Madikeri. Residents of Madikeri took part in the various poojas. A small silver Shiva-linga belonging to Subarasaiah was placed within the sanctum sanctorum. Lingarajendra also arranged for a lamp to be lit in perpetuity inside the temple. This practice continues to this day.

Lingarajendra finally did get some psychological relief from the ghost of Subarasaiah after the Omkareshwara temple was built and consecrated. However, the curse of the Brahmin lingered. The spectre of Subarasaiah returned to torture the mind of Lingarajendra. His mental and physical health steadily deteriorated. By the end of the same year, Lingarajendra died a troubled soul at the age of forty-five.

HALERI RAJAS AND THE BRITISH

After the signing of the strategic friendship treaty by Dodda Veerarajendra with the British East India Company in 1790, there were regular interractions between the officers of the Company and the rajas of Coorg. Even though the treaty was primarily signed to jointly fight their common enemy, Tipu Sultan of Mysore, the British treated Coorg as a protectorate. After Tipu's elimination in 1799, the Wodiyars were reinstated, and the kingdom of Mysore too came under British control. Their resident at Mysore was given charge of overseeing Coorg.

It was in around 1795–1801 that Dodda Veerarajendra built a guest house exclusively for his frequent British visitors. The building was very much in the architectural style of European structures. There are several mentions of this guest house in the writings of British visitors to Coorg. This accommodation had all the amenities the Europeans were accustomed to. A water-colour sketch by artist John Johnson gives a very realistic picture of this imposing structure, which unfortunately does not exist anymore. In the sketch, Mercara Fort can be seen in the background.

Lingarajendra improved upon this building and the surroundings. He added many facilities to suit the taste of his British guests. One of the guests, General James Welsh, who visited Coorg in 1811 during Lingarajendra's rule, as narrated earlier, gave the following graphic description of the building

Guest House for the British, Madikeri

where he and Lieutenant Williamson were accommodated:

> I must now describe our own habitation, built on a small island, surrounded by paddy ground, now dry for the sole accommodation of Europeans. It is a large square, having a hall in the centre, a large covered-in verandah all round it, and four bed-rooms projecting at the angles of the verandah, all on an upper story, the lower rooms serving for the guard, attendants, store-rooms etc. It stands on a square of seventy feet, the verandah having thirty-eight glass windows, with venetian blinds outside. The bed-rooms have sixteen windows, and the hall eight glass doors; every part being neatly furnished, in the English style, with beds, tables, card-tables, writing boxes, chairs, chandeliers, settees etc. etc. And there is an old butler of my Vellore friend Colonel Ridgway Mealay, and a dozen

active servants, who very speedily produce an English breakfast or dinner, served up on handsome Queen's ware, with every kind of European liquor; and what is even still more extraordinary, the cook bakes good bread!

Another visitor, Dr William Jeaffreson, was a guest of Chikka Veerarajendra, in 1830. He spent 22 days in Coorg.

Dr Jeaffreson was sent to Coorg by the British governor of Bombay, on Chikka Veerarajendra's request, to treat him for a rare disease. However, the raja had recovered by the time Dr Jeaffresson arrived in Coorg. Chikka Veerarajendra and the amiable Dr Jeaffreson became good friends and the raja requested the doctor to spend a few days in Coorg as his guest. The doctor was entertained with spectacular hunting expeditions during his stay. Dr Jeaffreson took many valuable trophies on his return to Bombay and was highly appreciative of the unforgettable experience and the warm hospitality extended by the raja. Later when Veerarajedra was exiled, and also during his stay in England, Dr Jeaffreson helped the raja in various ways, especially in his attempt to recover the investments made by his uncle Dodda Veerarajendra with the East India Company. Dr Jeaffreson was the author of the book *Coorg and its Rajas*, published in 1857. He genuinely felt that the last raja of Coorg was dealt unfairly by the British administration.

He wrote about the guest house in these lofty words:

…There we found a splendid bungalow, fitted up for our accommodation, with every possible convenience.

Round this residence grew flowers of the richest hues and the sweetest perfume, while trees, laden with delicious fruit, among whose branches perched wild birds of the brightest and most variegated plumage, cast over us their agreeable shade.

Near this bungalow was a tank, made of black marble of the highest polish and most elaborate workmanship, in the centre of which rose a fountain, throwing up jets of water so clear and pellucid that hundreds of large and beautiful fish might be seen disporting in the basin, or else darting about in every direction after their prey. This tank was the favourite resort of the Rajah who was wont to visit it daily, at noon. Standing beside it, he would ring a small gold bell, he carried in his hand, and, at its tinkling, all the fish collected together at one spot, anxiously waiting their food (young frogs, parched peas etc.), which an attendant threw to them from a basket.

In another part of the garden was an immense black marble stand, of pyramidal form, along the five front steps of which were arranged hundreds of bleached skulls of elephants, being the *Spolia Opima* of the chase.

After the British annexed Coorg in 1834, this building was surprisingly neglected. By 1860s it was in ruins. It was in 1862 that sixty-four Coorg elders approached the British government for assistance in constructing a boarding school for boys. They suggested the site of the guest house for the school and the hostel, and further requested the material from the collapsed building be used for the construction. The British agreed, and all the required facilities were ready by 1871 under Rev. G. Richter's supervision. Rev. Richter served as its principal for several years. The more than 140-year-old Central School is now a junior college and continues to be as vibrant as ever.

DEWAN KUNTA BASAVA'S ROLE IN THE FALL OF HALERI DYNASTY

During the reign of Dodda Veerarajendra, Lingarajendra had kept away from his domineering brother and was quite happy leading a peaceful life at his farm in Haleri. He was happiest hunting and maintaining his stables and kennels.

A young lad, named Basava, was one of the caretakers of his kennel. Basava was a faithful servant and accompanied Lingarajendra during his hunts in the forest. Though illiterate and crude in his behaviour, Basava was efficient, loyal and catered to all the demands of his master. He grew up to be a tall and powerfully-built young man. Over a period of time, Basava became a confidant and henchman of Lingarajendra. During one of the hunting expeditions, Basava was seriously injured and broke one of his legs. After this accident, he walked with a limp.

Following the death of Dodda Veerarajendra in 1809, Lingarajendra successfully sidelined his young niece Devammaji who was anointed queen of Kodagu. Subsequently, he usurped the throne in 1811. With Lingarajendra in power, the influence of Basava grew exponentially. Basava was made a sepoy and given the responsibility of looking after Chikka Veerarajendra, the young son and heir-apparent of Lingarajendra.

The increasing authority of Basava in decision-making caused great resentment in the court of Lingarajendra. Basava

Chikka Veerarajendra

was rapidly elevated from a sepoy to jamedar to the senior position of kariakara or an army commander. Many respected dewans and kariakaras were insulted and humiliated by this one time dog keeper of Lingarajendra. Basava was hated, and because of his limp people referred to him derogatorily as Kunta Basava or Basava the Lame. On Basava's advice, Lingarajendra put to death many senior officials in his court on charges of treason. At Kunta Basava's instigation, Lingarajendra also resorted to the infamous 'kuthinasa'—destruction to the roots—of some of the families.

During the last years of Lingarajendra's reign, Basava was elevated to the position of dewan. His heir-apparent Chikka Veerarajendra also grew up under the influence of Basava's evil machinations. When Chikka Veerarajendra ascended the throne in 1820, Basava became his most trusted dewan as well as sounding board. The other three elder dewans namely Dewan Chepudira Ponnappa, Dewan Apparanda Bopanna and Dewan Laxminarayana were marginalized. Chikka Veerarajendra was barely eighteen years of age when he became the king of Kodagu in 1820. Like his father, he too was more comfortable in the company of his childhood friend Dewan Basava, and other sycophants. Dewan Basava was the power behind the throne and no one could stop him from his nefarious activities.

Basava was the primary cause for Chikka Veerarajendra's unpopularity amongst his subjects. As soon as Chikka Veerarajendra ascended the throne, he had a large number of his close family members murdered to prevent any threat to his reign. He was highly suspicious of his uncle, Dodda Veerarajendra's four daughters. With Dewan Basava's conspiracy, twenty-eight members of the second daughter of Dodda Veerarajendra, Muddammaji and her Kodava husband Palaganda Chennaveerappa, were eliminated in a single day.

Chikka Veerarajendra was, above all, highly apprehensive of his cousin, the erstwhile rani, Devammaji. Similar to the apprehensions of his father Lingarajendra, he too feared his subjects rallying round Devammaji to reinstate her as the queen. With Dewan Basava's connivance, he planned to eliminate Devammaji. Before executing this wicked plan, he wanted to take possession of the fabled jewellery and gems that Devammaji's late father had bequeathed to her. Consequently, he lured Devammaji and her sister Mahadevammaji to Madikeri and kept them under virtual house arrest in the fort. Dewan Kunta Basava confronted Devammaji: 'Tell me where the royal treasure is hidden if you want to remain alive.' Under persistent mental torture and death threat by Dewan Basava, Devammaji revealed the hiding place of the treasure. She imprudently believed that her life would be spared in exchange for the fortune. Sadly, it proved to be just the opposite. Once the secret was releaved, Dewan Basava pitilessly hanged, with his own hands, both Devammaji and Mahadevammaji even as they pleaded with him to spare their lives. The third daughter of Dodda Veerarajendra died prematurely of illness, and thus the lineage of Dodda Veerarajendra came to a gruesome end.

Chikka Veerarajendra had another equally uncouth advisor in his court, a corpulent Muslim called Abbas Ali from Mysore. Dewan Kunta Basava and Abbas Ali collaborated in committing atrocities on the leading families in Kodagu. The common citizen too suffered because of bad governance. News of the increasing number of murders in Kodagu at the behest of Dewan Basava and Abbas Ali reached the British. They had also received complaints from some of the family members of the raja. By then James Archibald Casamajor had succeeded Arthur Cole as the resident at Mysore and was now the ex-officio resident of Coorg. Casamajor sent one of his assistants, Captain Monk, to Coorg in 1826 to enquire about reports of murders of Dodda Veerarajendra's family. Chikka Veerarajendra glossed over the issue with the explanation that an outbreak of cholera had claimed the lives of the late raja's family. Casamajor himself made a trip to Coorg in November 1826 and confronted the young raja with reports of atrocities. Chikka Veerarajendra denied every charge. Casamajor, though not convinced, gave a rather favorable account of the raja to his superiors.

By early 1830, Chikka Veerarajendra targeted his sister, also named Devammaji, and her Kodava husband Mukkatira Chennabasappa, suspecting them of plotting against his rule. He and his favourite dewan planned the assassination of Devammaji and her husband. They somehow got wind of the malicious intentions of the king and managed to escape to neighbouring Mysore for safety. At Mysore they sought refuge with the British, and Casamajor offered them temporary asylum. Chikka Veerarajendra was infuriated and demanded their immediate repatriation to Coorg. The British refused and this led to a confrontation between Chikka Veerarajendra and the British. In retaliation, Kunta Basava instigated the raja to murder Chennabasappa's brother Muddayya who was a senior and trusted official in the raja's court. Kunta Basava, in the process, eliminated a potential rival to him in the raja's court.

Casamajor made another visit to Coorg in January 1833 and had lengthy discussions with the raja. Chikka Veerarajendra promised to mend his ways, but soon resorted to atrocities on his subjects. He demanded the return of his sister and brother-in-law who were given protection by the British in Mysore.

Again in 1933, the British sent two of their native emissaries to investigate the allegations of numerous tortures and killings in Kodagu at the behest of the raja and his cohorts. Chikka Veerarajendra was by then on a collision course with the British on Dewan Basava's advice. The emissaries, Kulapally Karunakaran Menon and Dara Seth, were recklessly imprisoned by the raja. This action further deteriorated the relationship between the East India Company and the raja of Kodagu. When the British warned him, the raja released Dara Seth but kept Kulapally Menon as hostage and conveyed to the British that he would be released in exchange for his sister Devammaji and her husband Chennabasava.

Chikka Veerarajendra remained defiant and continued his nefarious activities adroitly assisted by Dewan Basava and Abbas Ali. At this point in time, a Sikh named Lahore Singh visited Kodagu. He extolled about the immense power of Maharaja Ranjit Singh who ruled vast areas of the northwest including parts of present day Afghanistan, from his capital in Lahore. Even the British were wary of Ranjit Singh. The raja contemplated an outlandish scheme on the advice of Dewan Basava and

Dewan Chepudira Ponnappa

other sycophants. The raja seriously considered an alliance with Maharaja Ranjit Singh, popularly known as the 'Lion of Punjab', against the British. When the sheer distance between Kodagu and Khandahar was explained, this delusion evaporated. However, the alliance that the raja of Kodagu sought with the maharaja of Punjab was to resurface in quite an unexpected saga to be enacted many years later at the heart of the British Empire—London!

By the end of 1933, Chikka Veerarajendra was totally at loggerheads with the British. Dewan Basava and Abbas Ali convinced the raja that with the guerrilla tactics of the Kodagu army, they could effectively outsmart the East India Company even though the British were well-entrenched in Mysore by then. 'After all,' they foolishly reasoned with the gullible raja, 'the Kodagu army effectively thwarted Tipu's soldiers in the past, and were equally capable of dealing with the feringhees.'

In spite of repeated appeals, the raja refused to release Kulapally Karunakaran Menon. Menon cautioned the raja of the futility of crossing swords with the British as they were in a position to 'muster more troops than there are trees in Kodagu.'

The impasse between the British and Chikka Veerarajendra

continued, and in February 1834, the then governor general of India, Lord William Bentinck himself wrote a letter to the raja requesting him to immediately release their representative Menon, or face the consequences of the old friendship treaty between Kodagu rajas and the British being revoked. Dewan Basava prompted the raja to respond aggressively to the British. Chikka Veerarajendra wrote a highly provocative proclamation intended to rally the 'Hindus, Muslims, peasants, merchants, and people of other castes in Hindustan to rise against the foreigners who were on a mission to convert the people of this land to their religion.' Copies of this proclamation were distributed in the neighbouring areas as well.

Regardless of the exaggerated prowess of the Haleri dynasty that Dewan Basava tried to project before the king, Chikka Veerarajendra himself started feeling vulnerable and unsure of the outcome of a military confrontation with the British. He summoned his senior dewan—Chepudira Ponnappa—to the court to get his views on the conflict with the British.

Dewan Ponnappa, who had served in the courts of the raja's uncle Dodda Veerarajendra and father Lingarajendra, was very frank in his advice. He appealed to the raja not to provoke the British to an armed conflict since their military power was far superior than that of the kingdom of Kodagu. He urged Chikka Veerarajendra to immediately release Kulapally Karunakaran Menon unconditionally and defuse the tension. Dewan Basava who was also present at the court was furious. In his rage, he struck Dewan Ponnappa. The powerful blow to his head knocked the seventy-one-year-old dewan to the ground and he briefly lost consciousness. Dewan Ponnappa staggered and got back on his feet. He bowed to the raja, and without uttering another word, left the court.

By early 1834, it was apparent that the British would launch an attack on Kodagu. The East India Company mobilized their troops from Mysore in the east, and Kannur in the southwest. Governor General Lord William Bentinck set out from Calcutta on 3 February 1834 on board the *Curacoa* to Madras on official duty, and one of his agendas was to coordinate military action against the raja of Coorg. British commander-in-chief of the Madras Army, Lt Gen. Sir Robert O'Callaghan was also in attendance. William Bentinck came down to Mysore, and after extensive discussions with Casamajor, declared war on Coorg on 15 March 1834 while he was on his way to Ooty. The military action was carried out under the overall command of Brigadier Lindsay who was instructed to execute the operation swiftly and complete the take-over of Coorg well before the onset of monsoon.

Chikka Veerarajendra issued another proclamation urging all his subjects to be ready for war. On the advice of Dewan Basava, some of the surviving members of the royal family were put to death so that the British would not find any relatives of the Haleri dynasty to replace Chikka Veerarajendra. These treacherous actions of Dewan Basava including the assault on Dewan Ponnappa further alienated a large number of Kodavas.

Chikka Veerarajendra on his part moved to the safety of Nalaknad Palace accompanied by his wives and Dewan Kunta Basava. He ordered his men to build roadblocks and fell large trees all along the way. When the enemy troops started moving into Kodagu, Chikka Veerarajendra realized his folly and lost his nerve. He sent Dewan Laxminarayana to seek peace with the

British. He also made immediate arrangements for the release of Kulapally Karunakaran Menon. However, it was a little too late. The British were not going to give up this opportunity, and demanded an unconditional surrender of the raja.

In the meantime, Dewan Ponnappa and Dewan Bopanna who were in Madikeri did not take part in resisting the invasion of Kodagu by the British. They and their followers decided that it would be prudent to surrender to the British and unseat the unpopular raja from the throne of Kodagu. Accordingly, on 5 April, Dewan Bopanna accompanied by four hundred men marched to Kushalnagar where Col J.S. Fraser, the political agent of the East India Company was camping, and communicated their desire to surrender to the British. Dewan Bopanna escorted Col Fraser to Madikeri.

Four columns of the British troops moved into Kodagu from different directions. They encountered scattered resistance from some of the loyal troops of the raja. By the evening of 6 April, the troops under the command of Col Stewart reached Madikeri, and occupied the fort without any resistance. The British flag was hoisted on the ramparts of the Madikeri Fort to the report of twenty-one blasts from cannons. A message was sent to Chikka Veerarajendra to surrender to the British within three days.

The raja and his entourage of two thousand men, along with his family reached Madikeri from Nalaknad on 10 April. The British, to avoid stirring passions of the citizens of Kodagu, diplomatically received their king and his family with full state honours at the entrance to Madikeri Fort. Once inside the fort, Chikka Veerarajendra was held hostage in his own palace.

The British now wanted Dewan Basava to be captured.

They announced a thousand rupees reward for his arrest. Many Kodavas were keen on getting even with Dewan Basava. A large number of them went looking out for the fugitive in the forests around Nalaknad Palace.

Earlier, Dewan Basava had requested a final meal of the leftovers of raja's household at Nalaknad Palace before Chikka Veerarajendra departed to Madikeri. A meal with the raja, of the leftovers from the palace kitchen, was considered a rare honour. It was known as 'edde bojana'. He took leave of his master and disappeared into the forest and knew very well that his days were numbered, and that his enemies would soon come hunting for him. Being lame, he could not move quickly. On 15 April 1834, Dewan Basava was found dead in the forest hanging from a tree.

Coorg thus became the only territory to be annexed by the British East India Company during the tenure of Lord William Bentinck (1828–1835), who was otherwise preoccupied in reforming and abolishing some of the horrendous social practices in India.

CHIKKA VEERARAJENDRA'S EXILE

On 6 April 1834, the sun finally set on the 234-year rule (1600–1834) of Kodagu by the Haleri dynasty of Lingayat rajas. The eastern column of the British troops advanced from Kushalnagar to Madikeri and reached the fort at 4 in the evening. Colonel J.S. Fraser, who accompanied the expedition as the political agent of Governor General Lord William Bentinck, took charge of the administration. In accordance with the British ultimatum, Chikka Veerarajendra travelled from Nalaknad Palace along with his wives, family and servants, and surrendered at Madikeri in the forenoon of 10 April.

In a proclamation issued by Col Fraser on 11 April 1834, the people of Kodagu were informed that the British had permanently replaced Chikka Veerarajendra's rule. Colonel Fraser advised the entire officialdom that worked for the raja to approach him for any matter concerning the administration of the land.

Chikka Veerarajendra, now a captive of the British, requested Col Fraser for a meeting with him. On the evening of 11 April, Col Fraser met the raja in the palace. All the windows of the palace were shut to prevent the guards of the 39th Regiment of the British army surrounding the fort from looking into the private chambers of the raja and his family. The rooms were kept dark with the drapes drawn, and Col Fraser had to grope his way along. A despondent Chikka Veerarajendra held the colonel's hand and took him to a room upstairs. They had discussions till well past 7 in the evening. They conversed in faltering Hindustani. Col Fraser subtly informed the raja that he would not be allowed to live in Kodagu. He briefed him about his impending deportation out of his kingdom.

Chikka Veerarajendra realized his monumental blunders in taking on an adversary far too stronger, and he made vain attempts at blaming all the wrongdoings on his dewan Kunta Basava and confidant Abbas Ali. He also realized his folly in alienating his own subjects. Chikka Veerarajendra did not expect the British to exile him out of his kingdom. Initially, he had hoped he would be allowed to dwell in the palace at Madikeri. When Col Fraser categorically rejected this, he requested to be allowed to live either at Nalaknad or in Periapatna. The British had already decided on keeping the raja well away from Kodagu. It was their policy to pre-empt the supporters of deposed rulers from regrouping and creating problems for the Company in future. This drastic decision of the British to banish their deposed king out of the kingdom shocked the citizens of Kodagu. The citizenry were overtaken by the events, and the age-old belief of rajas being divine representatives as propounded by Manu still lingered. An emotional representation was made by a section of the population to allow the king to live in Kodagu under the administration of the British. After a meeting with Col Fraser, the Kodava elders realized that they had no choice but to concur with the uncompromising decision of the British in the deportation of the raja and his family. Majority of the people of Kodagu expressed their desire to be ruled by the laws and regulations that prevailed in other dominions of the East India Company. Col Fraser, in a proclamation issued on 7 May 1834 assured the citizens of Kodagu that the British would respect the civil customs and religious practices of the people and that the new administration would provide security as well as ensure peace in the land. He also allayed their fears of the deposed raja ever returning to Kodagu and inflicting any kind of retribution on them.

On 24 April 1834, the thirty-two-year-old raja, his family and personal staff left Madikeri Fort at 3 in the afternoon. Chikka Veerarajendra, however, still entertained the hope of returning to his kingdom some day in the future. The entourage included thirteen of his wives and a two-year-old son named Chitrashekara born to one of his minor wives. Chikka Veerarajendra put up a brave front, and ceremoniously rode on an elephant out of the fort, dressed in his royal regalia. The British disdainfully arranged for a 21-gun salute to the raja. Veerarajendra quite thoughtlessly asked the palace band to play the joyful tune of 'The British Grenadiers', as his elephant sauntered along the streets of Madikeri. It was surreal and in total contrast to the humiliating moment when a king was being exiled from his kingdom. The streets were crowded with curious and confused citizens. The entire population of Madikeri stood along the route not knowing whether to mourn or to rejoice. While some shed tears at the departure of their raja, those who suffered at his hands were happy to see him banished.

Seventy-seven female members of the entourage travelled in bullock cart carriages and palanquins. As the palanquin bearers of the thirteen queens were struggling with their burden, someone in the crowd made a wisecrack: 'Looks like all the wives of the raja are pregnant!' Ten bullock carts followed, carrying the royal household effects. There were a dozen cooks, twenty personal attendants and fifty unarmed Coorgs. At the border of the town, Chikka Veerarajendra dismounted from the elephant and got onto his horse. He rode on horseback for about an hour. As the sun went down the hills, depression set in and he got into his palanquin for the onward journey. Many loyal citizens of the raja followed the procession. It was a sad spectacle. To add to the melancholy, dark clouds gathered. Soon, there was a downpour forcing the people following the entourage to return to their homes. It was an ignominious end to the two-century-old dynasty of Haleri rajas.

Col Stewart, who led a sub-division of the eastern column, was assigned the duty of accompanying Chikka Veerarajendra during the journey from Madikeri to Bangalore. In addition, one Capt. T.D. Carpenter was appointed as the agent of the governor general, in charge of the raja. A posse of British soldiers on horseback, assisted by sepoys from the Mysore army, escorted the royal family and their servants. Elaborate instructions were issued from Madras on how to conduct the transportation of the raja and his retinue. Of utmost priority to the British was the safety of the raja and the women accompanying him. Whenever they halted on the way, the soldiers and other officers were instructed not to go anywhere near the marquees of the raja and his family, and to respect their privacy. However, the only person to have access to Chikka Veerarajendra's tent at all times was Col Stewart. The entire camping site was to be cordoned off by the British soldiers, and none to be allowed to either enter or exit the camp.

Whilst the raja and his family were transported in their comfortable palanquins, the rest of the entourage travelled in bullock carts loaded with royal household belongings. Chikka

Veerarajendra was allowed to take 10,000 rupees for expenses during the journey. The British had confiscated valuables worth 16 lakh rupees besides all his other assets. A 'prize agent' was appointed to distribute this amount amongst the British soldiers and officers who took part in the annexation of Kodagu. However, the raja concealed a great deal of gold coins and jewellery in the palanquins of his wives. This was the reason why the palanquin bearers found the load unbearably heavy. The entourage camped near Kushalnagar for three days. The palanquin bearers complained about the heavy load and the problems they faced walking on the waterlogged road. A few of them managed to slip out of the camp and run away. Chikka Veerarajendra had no choice but to reduce the weight of the palanquins. In the middle of the night, he with the help of some of his loyal attendants secretly dug deep pits within the confines of the tents and buried several sacks full of gold and silver coins.

While at the camp, the raja also had an elaborate pooja performed by a well-known purohit and astrologer named Harangi Narasimha Sastri for his and his family's well-being.

The royal entourage reached Bangalore on 12 May 1834 after halting at various camps en route, including Mysore. Col Stewart formally handed over the deposed raja to the British Commissioner of Mysore Territories at Bangalore. In the meantime, one of the Kodava kariakaras who accompanied the raja till Bangalore allegedly helped himself to some of the buried treasure on his way back to Kodagu. When news of the hidden treasure leaked out, he hastened to inform the British of the spot where the gold and silver were hidden. The British immediately sent a team to unearth the valuables. Most of the buried sacks of coins were recovered. The informer got a reward of 1,000 rupees, and got to keep what he had surreptitiously pocketed earlier! But rumours persisted of more hidden treasures in other camping sites of the exiled king.

After about a month at Bangalore, the raja, his family and servants were taken to Vellore. On reaching Vellore on 6 July 1834, they were housed in a well-appointed accommodation within the Vellore Fort where the British had earlier detained the raja of Kandy from Sri Lanka. Chikka Veerarajendra lived in Vellore till March 1835, and was granted a monthly pension of 6,000 rupees out of the revenue from Kodagu. Two more sons named Lingaraja and Somashekara were born to his royal consorts during his stay at Vellore. However, the change in the environment took its toll. One of his principal wives and a newly born infant died. Two women in his entourage also fell victims to diseases. The British were not too happy with the frequent visitors the raja received from Kodagu. To forestall any rallying of support for Chikka Veerarajendra, he and his family were permanently exiled to Benares. They reached Benares in late February 1836. He was virtually under house arrest at Benares, with the British keeping a close watch on all his activities. The British named the haveli where the raja lived as 'Coorg Nest'.

Chikka Veerarajendra lived in Benares for fourteen years. During his stay in the holy city, he was able to live a comfortable life using the wealth he had brought with him. He retained most of the large retinue of cooks, attendants and servants from Kodagu. The monthly pension of 6,000 rupees that he received from the British allowed him considerable luxury though nowhere close to what he enjoyed in his own kingdom.

Chikka Veerarajendra made a few attempts at establishing contact with people of Kodagu but without any success. The people of Kodagu were quite happy under the new dispensation. The last raja of the Haleri dynasty finally reconciled himself to life in exile.

While at Benares, four more sons—Virabhadra, Nanjunda, Mudduraja and Patamaraja were born to the raja. Out of seven sons, three died young. The remaining four lived at Benares and received a small stipend from the British after the death of Chikka Veerarajendra in 1859. They were interested in renewing their connections with Kodagu and made overtures at matrimonial alliance with girls from their former homeland. They sent emissaries to find out if any leading Kodava and Brahmin families would give their daughters in marriage to them. The Kodavas had not forgotten the misdeeds of their former ruler, and flatly refused to have any association with the raja's family. Chikka Veerarajendra's favourite daughter Gowramma was born on 4 July 1841 at Benares to one of his royal consorts who died at childbirth. Chikka Veerarajendra was highly protective of his orphaned daughter. Three more daughters were born to other wives of the raja. One of them named Gangamma was fair and pretty. While she was still young, Jung Bahadur, a member of the ruling

Chikka Veerarajendra in royal regalia in Benares

family of Nepal, saw her during a visit to Benares. Smitten, he married princess Gangamma when she was barely a teenager.

The British, firmly established in Kodagu, set-up their administrative offices within the fort complex at Madikeri. They anglicized the name of Kodagu to Coorg and that of Madikeri to Mercara. And Kodavas came to be known as Coorgs. These anglicized names are still popular.

KONGETTIRA RANI KAVERAMMAJI

It was the girls' task to fetch water every day before dusk from the crystal clear stream that gushed down the hills. Kaveramma and her cousins laughed and splashed water merrily on one another near the falls as they filled their vessels. Their village, Chettalli, was famous for spring water that cascaded spectacularly from the high mountaintops. They were a giggly bunch of four teenagers teasing each other about the crush they had on that handsome young man, Gappu, from the neighbouring village. They had seen Gappu at a recent wedding when he had come along with the groom's party to their Kongettira Ainmane. Kavery had overheard her parents talk about Gappu being a good match for her. By the time they got back home, the girls were totally drenched. It was already dark. They hurried to their dimly-lit rooms to quickly change before the elders reprimanded them. Kaveramma's mother sat in a corner of the room and was preoccupied with nursing her six-month-old infant son.

There was a visitor in the house, and all the elders were sitting with him in the courtyard discussing about the raja. They spoke in hushed tones about the atrocities being committed by Chikka Veerarajendra and his coterie. The name of Dewan Kunta Basava was mentioned repeatedly as being the worst influence on the naive raja. The girls were shocked and confused when they heard that the raja had ordered every lactating mother to supply breast milk to the royal kitchen. On the advice of his astrologers Chikka Veerarajendra drank human milk, and had his favourite payasam prepared with it. The visitor advised the parents to keep their unmarried daughters well out of sight and reach of this sinful raja.

A few days later, Kaveramma and her cousins learnt that Chikka Veerarajendra would be passing through their village the following day on his way to Kushalnagar. While the village headman and other prominent citizens were duty bound to welcome the raja and his staff, they instructed their teenage daughters to stay indoors. The girls were, however, curious and wanted to see the raja ride past their village.

A pandal was erected at the entrance to the village and the elders waited with garlands, fresh fruits and refreshments for the raja and his team. A man on horseback came and announced that the raja would be reaching the village within an hour. Kavery and her cousins sneaked out of their house and blended with the people standing on either side of the road.

Dressed in his royal regalia, Chikka Veerarajendra rode into Chettalli on a magnificent white horse with black patches. He was handsome and imperious. An empty palanquin followed, hauled by four men, which was to carry the raja if he was tired of riding the steed.

Kaveramma and her friends were overawed by this spectacle. They edged past the crowd for a better look, and that was when Chikka Veerarajendra's eyes fell on the fair, sharp-featured Kavery. The raja suddenly pulled back his horse and stared at the awestruck girl. One of his officials rushed to the raja's side. Chikka Veerarajendra dismounted to meet his subjects. While receiving their offerings, he instructed his assistant to find out about the beautiful young girl. He wanted an alliance worked out by the time he was on his way back to Madikeri three days later.

None in the Kongettira clan was happy with this development. Kaveramma was totally confused and unhappy. She dreamt of being handsome Gappu's wife. She had not heard any good word about the raja. Kaveramma knew that she would be converted to the Lingayat sect and would not return to her beloved Chettalli, her family, and friends. There was a deep sense of foreboding in the Kongettira Ainmane. There was no way the raja's orders could be defied. After much debating, the elders set a condition. They told the raja's representatives: 'Our daughter will be betrothed to the raja only if she is taken as one of his principal wives.' When this was mentioned to Chikka Veerarajendra, he readily agreed.

Consequently, a reluctant Kaveramma was taken to Madikeri. She was made to go through a series of ceremonies to convert her to a Lingayat. The young Kavery kept weeping through all the rituals.

The marriage took place while the pre-monsoon rain drizzled on Madikeri. She was now respectfully called Kaverammaji, and had six women servants at her beck and call. The dwelling place in the royal zenana too had all the comforts. However, the adolescent girl, uprooted from her environment, was most unhappy. She missed her playmates and her familiar surroundings. Though living in the palace, young Kavery was intimidated by the eunuchs who guarded the harem. She found them crude and repulsive.

Whenever the raja visited Kaverammaji, he showered her with gifts and expensive jewellery. After a few months of her marriage, she reconciled to her fate. She found the raja to be kind and considerate towards her. He didn't seem as bad as the rumours she had heard earlier. Chikka Veerarajendra admired her intelligence, strong will and determination. Kaverammaji liked visiting the Nalaknad Palace and its surroundings. It reminded her of her cherished days at Chettalli.

Chikka Veerarajendra, however, continued to be unpopular among his subjects. His dependence on Dewan Kunta Basava was proving to be too costly for him. By the 1830s, reports of his atrocities against the daughters of his uncle Dodda Veerarajendra reached the British Resident Arthur Cole at Mysore. This provided them with a good excuse to interfere in the affairs of Coorg citing misrule by Chikka Veerarajendra.

Kaverammaji realized the seriousness of the developments only when the entire royal household shifted to Nalaknad Palace at short notice. By April 1834, the beleaguered raja was forced to surrender to the British, and was soon exiled from his kingdom.

For Kaveramma, this was a shock she could not come to terms with. Being away from Chettalli was traumatic enough. Now to be away from Kodagu was incomprehensible. She wished she had remained an ordinary girl and lived a carefree life.

For their journey out of Kodagu, each of the thirteen wives was allotted a palanquin. The raja had instructed his queens to bundle all their jewellery and other valuables from the palace in their clothes and conceal them in the palanquin. This was far in excess of the gems, gold and jewellery that the British had permitted the raja to take from his kingdom. Chikka Veerarajendra was sure that the conquerors would not subject the women to any search.

The journey out of their homeland was most depressing

for the royal entourage. Even though the raja maintained a brave front, his consorts were frightened and some of them wailed loudly. It was heart-wrenching for Kavery as the convoy snaked its way through the winding roads near her childhood home in Chettalli. Women and children who stood along the way wept at the ignominious exit of their raja. The British officers and the soldiers firmly dissuaded the people from following the royal caravan. The entourage camped at two different places within the borders of Kodagu. At the first camp, most of the palanquin bearers complained about the heavy load and some of them absconded. To lighten the palanquins, the raja and his confidants buried part of the treasure in the darkness of night, at various spots within the tents that were pitched for them. The raja hoped to return one day to retrieve the valuables.

Kongettira Rani Kaverammaji

The journey to Bangalore and then on to Vellore was tedious. The dry summer heat was too much to bear. Once in Vellore, the raja, his wives and staff found the accommodation comfortable, but did not feel at home. Kavery and the other queens lived in the hope that they would soon return to Kodagu, and that the nightmare would end. But to their horror, within a year of residing at Vellore, they were told by the British to prepare themselves for travel again. Sensing that the raja might be emboldened to foment trouble, the British decided to transfer Chikka Veerarajendra and his family to distant Benares.

They undertook the long journey to Benares in March 1835. They first reached Madras, and from there travelled along the east coast in palanquins and bullock carts. By July, they reached Ganjam in Orissa. By then, the relentless summer heat had sapped their energy. Mercifully, the rains hit the region and Captain T.D. Carpenter, who was in charge of the royal entourage, arranged for the raja and his family to break journey in Ganjam until the end of the rainy season. Two separate houses were rented to accommodate the growing family of the raja.

Whenever Chikka Veerarajendra visited Kavery, her only query was to know when they were going back to Kodagu. The raja had to finally tell her that they would be permanently settled in Benares. She was devastated. By the time they resumed their journey it was December and winter had set in. The bitter cold accentuated her depression. The British arranged a comfortable and well-appointed haveli for the royal family and their assistants.

Kaverammaji and the other ranis were most uncomfortable with the weather and the environment in Benares. Having lived in the tranquil environment in Kodagu, they found Benares noisy and overcrowded with pilgrims. The raja was under house arrest and his movements were restrained. However, after a couple of years this restriction was relaxed, and Chikka Veerarajendra was allowed to visit various temples and holy places along with his wives and children. Over the years, he started making friends with the British officers and traders.

There were the occasional visitors from Kodagu who were permitted to meet the ex-raja, but only under British supervision. Chikka Veerarajendra eagerly sought news of his former kingdom. He learnt about the Amara-Sullya rebellion and how the British crushed it with help from his former dewans and kariakaras. Kaverammaji managed to send a message to her family in Chettalli that she was unhappy and desperately homesick.

When this news reached her parents, they were highly upset. They were in no position to travel to Benaras. Seeing their plight, three of their nephews—Nanjappa, Subbaiah and Medappa—came forward to make the arduous journey to meet their cousin Kavery, and also use the opportunity for a dip in the holy Ganges.

The three men from the Kongettira family set out on their pilgrimage a few days after the Puthari festival in December, circa 1841. The young men were given an emotional send-off by their clan members. It would be more than six months by the time they returned. The journey was fraught with danger. The notorious thugs stalked the travellers all along the route. The only gift that Kavery's parents could send for their daughter was a jar of her favourite bamboo-shoot pickle.

By the time the three Kongettira men reached Benares, walking all the way, the festival of Holi was being celebrated. There was great gaiety among the pilgrims, sadhus, mendicants and wandering minstrels, smearing colours on one another. Most of the people were high on opium and bhang. They witnessed strange behaviour by people, and at the same time there were the devout that visited temples and did poojas to atone for their sins. A few aged men and women had come to Benares to spend their last days, and to die on the banks of the holy river. After much searching, the trio located the large haveli

'Coorg Nest' where the raja and his queens resided.

The three cousins met Kavery at the appointed time and it was an emotional moment for all of them. They were meeting after more than twelve years, and much had changed since then. Kavery spoke to them from behind a screen. They could not see her face. Kavery eagerly enquired, 'How are Amma and Appa, and my little brother Boja?' She wanted to hear all about the other girls she had spent her childhood with. She could not resist dipping her fingers in the jar of pickle her parents had sent.

Kavery provided the visitors a guide from the royal household to take them to all the places of pilgrimage. They had the ritual dips in the Ganges and performed poojas on behalf of their relatives back home. They were mesmerized by the teeming humanity visiting the land of Lord Rama and Lord Krishna.

A month rolled by, and finally it was time for Nanjappa, Subbaiah and Medappa to return home. They went to take leave of Kaverammaji. The cousins knew that they would not meet again. Kavery wept behind the wooden trellis as she bid them farewell. She handed over valuable gifts for her parents and other close relatives and friends. She sent an ornate gold embroidered cap and a waistcoat for Boja. She handed them portraits of herself and the raja. She held a seed of a special variety of mango and told her cousins, 'Please plant this seed near the paddy fields in front of the ainmane where we used to catch crabs.' This was done in accordance with her wish. After a few years, it grew to be a mighty tree, and the fruits were luscious. The variety has been propagated and is now popularly known as Kongettira mango. (My grandmother, who belonged to the Kongettira family, used to tell us about having seen these gifts, and having tasted the mango from the original tree.)

As a final parting gift, Kavery whispered a secret to her three cousins. She told them about the places where the gold and silver coins were buried while the royal entourage were on their way out of Kodagu in that fateful summer of 1834.

By the time the three men returned, the monsoon rains lashed the countryside in Kodagu. On reaching home, they handed over the gifts from Kaverammaji, and spent the next two weeks narrating their experiences in Benares, and their adventures during the journey. Then one day, when the skies cleared, they set out to look for the buried treasure. Soon, the three men were richer by a few pots of gold and silver!

THE BRITISH IN COORG

The tactics that the British East India Company used to annex Coorg in 1834 were similar to what they employed, with repeated success, elsewhere in India as well. Their ruse was to claim that the rulers were despotic, debauched, repressive and inefficient. Ever since Dodda Veerarajendra signed the friendship treaty with the British in 1790, the Company kept a close watch on the kingdom of Coorg, gradually tightening their influence and grip over the rajas. In fact, the last three rajas were virtually under protectorate status of the British with the resident at Mysore having a say in the administration of Coorg. To make matters worse, the last king, Chikka Veerarajendra, provided sufficient fodder for the East India Company to substantiate a convenient case for taking total control over the administration of the tiny province. Besides, Chikka Veerarajendra had also alienated himself from his principal dewans and other high-ranking officers in his court. This led to the disgruntled dewans, kariakaras and karanikas in facilitating the white man to depose the unpopular raja. Chikka Veerarajendra perfectly fitted the stereotype that the British painted depicting the native rulers of India—that of an oriental despot. This helped them justify his overthrow and subsequent exile.

After the raja was banished from his kingdom, the citizens slowly reconciled to the rule of the new masters. The common man enjoyed more liberty under the new dispensation, and the law was more equitable than before. The British officers noticed that the people were quite appreciative of the changed order, and found them keen on improving their standard of living. The new administration focused on three core issues soon after Coorg came under their rule. The first was to provide schools for the education of the hitherto unlettered citizens of the land. The second was to teach the Gospel to 'enlighten' the heathen worshippers and to 'save' their souls. Finally, they promoted growing coffee for which the land and climate were ideally suited.

Colonel J.S. Fraser who took over as the administrator of Coorg, wisely continued the prominent positions held by most of those who served the raja's court. They retained the seventy-one-year-old Dewan Chepudira Ponnappa, and Dewan Apparanda Bopanna. They were consulted on all major policy decisions. Likewise, Kariakaras Biddanda Somayya and Kasi Thimmappa Gowda and a few others continued in their earlier positions. All these officers were given enhanced salaries and privileges. This ensured the loyalty of the Kodavas and other communities in Coorg. The general populace was further reassured when Colonel Fraser issued a proclamation on 7 May 1834 assuring the people that the British government would strive for their security, comfort and happiness.

Despite all these measures, a revolt erupted against the British in 1837 in Amara-Sullya, which was spearheaded by a jangama named Aparampara who claimed to be a descendant of the Haleri dynasty. However, when this spread to the borders of Coorg, a majority of the Kodavas did not support the uprising. With significant improvement in their living conditions, the Kodavas led by Dewan Apparanda Bopanna and

Dewan Chepudira Ponnappa, aided the British in crushing the uprising. One of the main leaders of the uprising, Guddemane Appaiah, was captured and hanged by the British at the Mercara Fort. Guddemane Appaiah is currently considered as one of the earliest freedom fighters against British rule. The Kodavas who helped the British in suppressing this uprising were rewarded handsomely. Later in 1857, the Kodavas again spontaneously came forward to fight for the British against the Sepoy Mutiny, which had engulfed the northern parts of the country. This demonstration of loyalty was appreciated, and Mark Cubbon, the chief commissioner of Mysore and Coorg, issued a notification in February 1861 exempting the Kodavas from the Disarming Act. After Independence, Kodavas and some other communities who owned land since the time of the rajas were exempted from sections 3 and 4 of the Indian Arms Act of 1959. It is important to note that this privilege has not been abused by the beneficiaries of the exemption.

Even though Col J.S. Fraser favoured proselytisation, he was wise not to use coercive methods, or to encourage overzealous evangelists. He donated a substantial portion of his 'prize money' for saving the souls of the people the British had liberated from a tyrant. He, however, reassured the various communities in Coorg that they were free to follow their religion, customs and cultural practices. In keeping with the sentiments of the population, he continued the ban on cow slaughter in Kodagu. These confidence-building measures did wonders in winning over the loyalty and cooperation of the people.

The British first opened an Anglo-vernacular school in Mercara and followed it by a Kannada school in Virajpet in

1835. Another school was subsequently started in Hudikeri. In the next twenty years, the number of vernacular schools in various parts of Coorg went up to twenty-one. Governor General Lord William Bentinck, who was deeply involved in bringing about reforms emphasized the teaching of the 'English language and general education, as panacea for regeneration of India'. It was indeed an example of 'enlightened self-interest' to have an educated cadre of Indians who could be employed to assist the British in the administration of this vast country.

However, till about 1855, these schools in Coorg provided rather basic education. Moreover, the quality of education was poor. Then in 1862, sixty-four elders from the Kodava community approached the British and expressed their desire to start a boarding school in Mercara with improved teaching facilities. They offered to partly finance the school project and requested the East India Company for substantial grant. The matter was taken up with The Earl of Elgin, the then governor general. The emphasis on educating the 'natives' was already given a strong impetus by Thomas Babington Macaulay when he arrived in India in 1834 as the law member. Consequently, the British administration was spontaneous in lending their support for starting the school in Mercara.

Construction of the Central High School in Mercara was started in 1863. As mentioned earlier, the site chosen for the school was close to where the European style guest house was located to accommodate and entertain the officers of the East India Company. This building, which was by then in a dilapidated condition, was brought down and the salvaged material was used for the construction of a school and boarding house for boys. It became fully functional by 1871 with Rev.

G. Richter as the principal. Subedhar Coluvanda Cariappa and Chepudira Subbaiah (an assistant commissioner in the British administration, and one of the grandsons of Dewan Ponnappa) were the two Kodavas who were actively involved in the school project. They were also instrumental in starting the 'Mercara School Endowment Plantation Fund' in 1863. Sadly, the plantation named 'School Estate' meant to generate funds for the school could not be run profitably. The plantation was sold, and the fund was renamed 'Coorg Education Fund' in the year 1916. Coorg Education Fund continues to be active, and over the years has helped thousands of Kodava boys and girls in their pursuit of education.

A job with the British government became an attractive proposition for the educated youth in India. The demand for learning encouraged more educational institutions to come up, and these were started mainly by the Christian missionaries. By the turn of the nineteenth century, there were quite a few prosperous Indian coffee planters in Coorg who could afford to send their children for higher education to Mysore, Mangalore, Bangalore and Madras. Within three decades, the Kodava community who were illiterate became an educated class, with equal emphasis given to educating their daughters as well. The British acknowledged the Kodavas as a martial race and encouraged them to join the armed forces. It was this initiative that made it possible for bright young men, during the 1920s, like Kodendera M. Cariappa and Kodendera S. Thimmaya (a direct descendant of Dewan Chepudira Ponnappa), to be selected for training in the elite Indian Military Academy and Sandhurst Military Academy in England respectively. Both of them distinguished themselves as chiefs of the Indian Army.

It's a matter of pride for Kodavas that the first woman to enter the Indian Foreign Service was from Kodagu—Chonira B. Muthamma.

The evangelists' expectation, that with education the Kodavas would automatically be attracted to the Christian faith, did not materialize. Much to their disappointment, the failure of the earlier attempt by Rev. Herman Moegling to convert the community was later reinforced by the dogged refusal of the Kodavas to move away from their age-old traditions. Even though during the rule of the Haleri rajas, the Kodavas were deeply influenced by the Hindu religion and are recognized as Hindus, they continued, and still continue ancestral worship practiced by the community for centuries. They became anglicized in their lifestyle but were steadfast in following their own faith. There was only limited success for the British in converting some of the poorer classes in Coorg to Christianity.

Riding on the success of education was the large-scale cultivation of coffee in Coorg. Coffee cultivation on a modest scale was already prevalent in Coorg, mainly by some of the Mapillas from Kerala. However, it was the British planters who came over from Sri Lanka who introduced the scientific cultivation of coffee. Some of the enterprising Kodavas and others soon found the cultivation of this plantation crop highly lucrative and took it up enthusiastically. Coffee cultivation was the single most important phenomenon which changed the socio-economic and cultural ethos of Kodagu and its inhabitants.

One of the first European planters was Fowler who started the Mercara Estate in 1850. Mann and Donald Stewart followed him in 1855, and started clearing the Sampaje Ghats to establish coffee plantations. Dr Maxwell subsequently opened

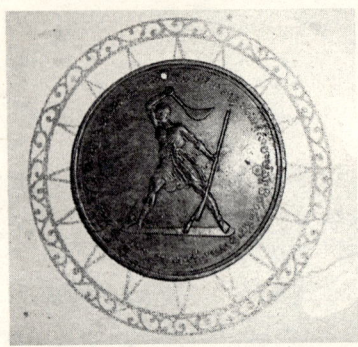 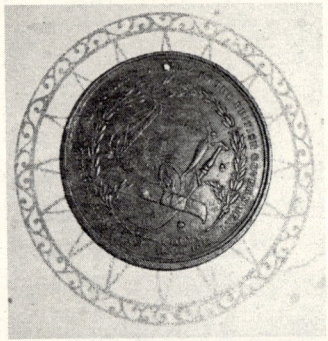

Sample of medals awarded by the British (obverse and reverse), 1837

the Perambadi Ghat Estates in 1856. Initially, some of these plantations were severely affected by pest attacks. It was then that it was realized that coffee grown under light shade with diffused sunlight fared better. This practice continues, and Indian coffee is specially marketed as a crop grown under natural tree cover which makes it environment-friendly.

Hundreds of Europeans were attracted to Coorg because of the favourable weather and the potential of starting and owning a coffee plantation. Many educated young men came to work as managers in these plantations. By the turn of the nineteenth century, there were about 130 European-owned coffee estates covering an area of 33,000 acres. Along with coffee, the estates were interspersed with pepper and oranges. Cardamom cultivation, which was already popular, was continued more scientifically now. All these crops improved the economy of Coorg significantly.

By the 1940s, the freedom movement had gained sufficient momentum in the country and became active in Coorg as well. The European planters feeling insecure started selling their plantations mainly to Kodavas, Mangaloreans and people from Kerala. By 1943, most of the remaining European owned plantations got together to form a public limited company known as Consolidated Coffee Ltd. This became the largest coffee estate in Asia. In 1997, the Tata group acquired the Consolidated Coffee Ltd and renamed it as Tata Coffee Ltd.

Some of the finest estate bungalows built by these planters in picturesque locations are still in good condition. The British, true to their traditions, started social clubs where they created 'Little England' exclusively for the whites. Three clubs started by the European planters—North Coorg Club (1883), Bamboo Club (1884) and Belur Club (1904)—are still active and are now used by the coffee planters of Coorg. These three clubs are listed amongst the hundred elite clubs of India.

CHRISTIANITY IN COORG

Roman Catholics first came to Coorg on the invitation of Veerarajendra in the year 1792. These were the 700 survivors out of the thousands of Christians from Mangalore, who were forcibly taken to Srirangapatana by Tipu Sultan. However, they managed to escape from Tipu's clutches after the third Anglo-Mysore war in 1792, but they could not go back to South Kanara since Tipu still held sway in Mangalore. Veerarajendra on the other hand wanted to repopulate his kingdom, which was depleted after the wars and abductions by the Sultan of Mysore. He founded Veerarajendrapette in 1792, and on the request of his new Christian subjects established the St Anne's Church in Virajpet. To help the cause, he also gave liberal grants in the form of land and financial support. After the British took over the administration of Coorg, this church received further boost and a school was also started in 1842.

The first chief commissioner of Coorg, Col J.S. Fraser, found the Coorgs to be an ideal group of people to embrace Christianity. He felt that, with education, Coorgs would automatically find the teachings in the Bible more attractive in comparison to their practice of heathen worship. However, there were instructions from the British government that religion should not be forced on Indians, and that their form of worship should not be interfered with. The administration in Coorg followed this policy during its first decade, which contributed to the acceptance of the British rule by a large percentage of the people. However, at the same time, missionaries were allowed to come and through gentle persuasion and inducements, voluntary conversions were permitted.

In the year 1852, Rev. Herman G. Moegling, the Mangalore-based German missionary, was preparing to leave for his native Germany for medical treatment when he had an unexpected visitor from Coorg—one Alamanda Somayya. The man was dressed as a sanyasi, and appeared to be in great distress. He requested Rev. Moegling to accept him into the Christian fold. Rev. Moegling was quite impressed by Somayya's commitment and felt it was a sort of divine intervention for initiating the spread of Christianity in Coorg. He cancelled his trip and decided to introduce the teachings of the Bible in Coorg through Somayya. Col Mark Cubbon who succeeded Col Fraser as the commissioner encouraged Rev. Moegling to establish the first Protestant church in Mercara in 1855 along with the Basel Mission School. (Both the church and the school are active to this day.)

Alamanda Somayya was a prominent Kodava and was a direct descendant of the famous Alamanda Doddavva. The Alamanda family owned large areas of land in Armeri village near Virajpet. Somayya and his brother had taken active part in supporting the British during the Amara-Sullya rebellion, which took place in 1837. In appreciation, the British rewarded them with grant of land and other perquisites.

In 1842, Somayya had undertaken an arduous journey to Benares to visit all the holy places, and also to meet the exiled king Chikka Veerarajendra. He lived in the north for three years and visited all the temples on the banks of Ganges as well as other holy places in the vicinity. After the pilgrimage, he returned to Coorg in 1845. His father Bollu had died when Somayya and his siblings were very young. Due to Somayya's preoccupation with religion, the cultivation of their land was neglected. In spite of the dire straits the family was in, Somayya and his brother arranged their own marriages in 1846. They had to borrow heavily for the ceremonies. They soon found that the earnings from their land were not sufficient to repay the loans and to sustain their families. Somayya started trading in cardamom to supplement his income. Misfortune struck when he lost money in this venture and his debts soared. In 1852, he was taken into custody by the government as a defaulter and kept in a jail in Kadanoor. On the third day of his captivity, Somayya escaped from prison. He left his wife and children at his in-laws' house and disappeared.

It was in this state that he approached Rev. Moegling in Mangalore. Rev. Moegling promised to help Somayya clear his debts. Somayya embraced Christianity and was baptized on 6 January 1853. He was given the name Stephanous Somayya. Rev. Moegling and his spiritual son Rev. Anandrao Kaundinya accompanied Somayya to Coorg in 1853. His wife and children were overjoyed on seeing him, and they too readily agreed and expressed their willingness to embrace Christianity. Rev. Moegling interpreted this initial success as: 'The first fruits of a small people hitherto untouched by Christianity.'

Rev. Moegling thereafter asked Somayya to take him and his companions to Armeri village. In Armeri, Rev. Moegling met the villagers and was accorded a warm welcome by the members of the Alamanda family. The missionary wanted a small house to be built on Somayya's land so that he could initiate teaching the Bible to those interested. By then, the news of Somayya's and his family's conversion to Christianity spread in the village. This enraged the villagers and they promptly disowned him and his family. At the same time the subedhar of the village, Mathanda Appachanna, declared that Somayya had lost his rights over the family property because of his conversion. Some of the Alamanda family members also threatened Stephanous Somayya. He was excommunicated from the community and forced to leave the village along with his wife, children and his brother's widow.

Consequently, Rev. Moegling provided them shelter in the travellers' bungalow in Virajpet and immediately sent a petition on behalf of Somayya to Chief Commissioner Col Mark Cubbon. The commissioner sought the opinion of leading Kodavas. The opinion of Sheristidhar Mandepanda Thimmayya, Naib Sheristidhar Bittianda Nanjappa and others was unanimous. They all stressed that by changing his religion, Stephanous Somayya had lost his rights over his family property. They also cautioned the British that encouraging conversion was against the assurances given to the Kodavas in 1834. This issue was referred to the governor general and it was later taken up in the civil court. The court ruled in favour of Somayya and passed an order that he would continue to enjoy the rights over his family property despite his conversion. Emboldened by the court ruling, Somayya returned to his land in Armeri, and as planned, Rev. Moegling built a small house next to Somayya's home. In 1854, Rev. Moegling also constructed a modest church on Somayya's land. About 130 labourers who constructed the priest's house and the church converted to Christianity along with their families. Later, one Manalachanda Poovakka and her son Ponnappa from Modoor village also embraced Christianity and joined Rev. Moegling's flock.

Meanwhile, tension in Armeri village continued since the Kodavas were very unhappy with the latest developments in their village. To add to their woes, the labourers who converted to Christianity now resented working for the Alamanda family. Rev. Moegling wrote to the chief commissioner and the superintendent of Coorg to grant him land so that he could settle the newly converted Christians there and develop a coffee estate. Accordingly, a plot of ninety-seven acres was granted for this settlement near Siddapur. Rev. Moegling deputed his adopted spiritual son, Rev. Anandrao Kaundinya, to develop the new settlement. In 1857, work was started by clearing the bamboo forest and building living quarters for the converts. A church was built and this new settlement was named 'Anandapura'. Most of this area is now part of the Anandapura Estate owned by Tata Coffee.

Rev. Herman Moegling continued as principal of the Lower Secondary School that he had started in Mercara around 1855. He made extensive study of Coorg and its history. His book *Coorg Memoirs* is one of the earliest documentations of history of Coorg. Stricken with ill-health, he left for Germany in 1860. He died there the same year.

Unable to stand the hostilities in Armeri, Stephanous Somayya and his family shifted to Anandapura. Under the supervision of Rev. Anandrao Kaundinya, about twenty-five acres of coffee estate was developed. This area was, however, infested with malaria, and there was constant sickness amongst the residents. By then misunderstanding crept between Rev. Kaundinya and Stephanous Somayya. Much to the consternation of Rev. Kaundinya, Somayya decided to renounce Christianity and return to his Kodava roots in Armeri!

After Rev. Kaundinya, Rev. Ferdinand Kittel managed Anandapura. Rev. Kittel, a German missionary, is well-known as the author of the Kittel's Kannada-English Dictionary. However, the Anandapura project had to be abandoned because of constant sickness amongst the workers on account of rampant malaria which the British referred to as 'Coorg Fever'.

Along with Somayya, there were just nine Kodavas who embraced Christianity. His son and two daughters shifted to Mangalore and continued as Christians. This entire project proved highly disappointing for the Protestant Mission.

Earlier, Rev. Moegling had another ambitious expectation. He hoped that the high profile Christian converts, Maharaja Duleep Singh of Punjab and Princess Victoria Gowramma of Coorg, would be united in holy matrimony and that they would come back to their domains to spread the Christian religion on a grand scale. The same dream, entertained by Queen Victoria and several British Evangelists, however, remained unfulfilled.

MAHARAJA DULEEP SINGH AND PRINCESS VICTORIA GOWRAMMA

Duleep Singh, the youngest son of Maharaja Ranjit Singh—the 'Lion of Punjab'—was born in 1838 to the maharaja's favourite and youngest wife Jindan Kaur. Princess Gowramma, the much-loved daughter of Chikka Veerarajendra—the last king of Coorg—was born in 1841 to one of his royal consorts while he was in exile in Benares. While Duleep Singh sat on the throne of Punjab briefly as a child-king with his mother as regent, Princess Gowramma never set foot on her native soil. The British East India Company had annexed both their territories. To prevent any rallying of support by their former subjects, the British artfully kept royalty well away from their respective homelands.

The paths of these two royal progeny were destined to cross. And had some of the plans the British intended for them worked, the history of India could have been significantly different.

The British took possession of Punjab in 1849. The following year, the twelve-year-old deposed maharaja was separated from his influential mother and exiled to Fatehgarh on the banks of the Ganges. One Dr John Spencer Login and his wife Lena Login, already familiar with India, were put in charge of looking after and tutoring the young maharaja. With clever indoctrination of the Gospels, the naive Duleep Singh gradually began to dislike his own religion. Soon he expressed his desire to embrace Christianity. By 1853, it was decided that the young maharaja was ready to be baptized. Governor General Dalhousie described the event as a 'remarkable event in history', and hoped that many other Indian royalties would follow suit.

However, a member of an Indian royal family had already converted to Christianity in 1852. Chikka Veerarajendra had obtained permission from the East India Company to visit England where he wished his favourite daughter, Gowramma, could have the advantage of a European education. To the delight of the British, the raja wanted his ten-year-old daughter to be brought up in accordance with the Christian faith. The raja, who had eleven children, referred to his daughter Gowramma as 'a pigeon amongst crows,' and 'the fairest amongst the flock'.

Chikka Veerarajendra and Gowramma arrived in London in May 1852. Chikka Veerarajendra was the first Indian royalty to arrive on the English soil. Two of his wives and a few servants also accompanied him. The directors of the East India Company accorded a highly publicized welcome to the raja and his young daughter. They soon became celebrities and were invited to lunches and dinners by the British high society.

Chikka Veerarajendra had another more important mission in London. His uncle Dodda Veerarajendra had invested large sums of money in the East India Company for the benefit of his daughter Devammaji who briefly sat on the throne of Coorg, and his other children. Lingarajendra had manipulated the British officers to draw the interest on theses investments during his reign, and his son Chikka Veerarajendra continued to enjoy this amount till 1833 when it was discovered by the British that Devammaji was brutally eliminated by Chikka Veerarajendra in

1832 as described in an earlier chapter. He now wanted the British to release the capital along with accrued interest, to him. Chikka Veerarajendra filed a suit at the Chancery Court against the East India Company for recovery of this amount citing himself as the only legal inheritor. Though the British had given him permission to reside in London only for a year, the legal suit prolonged his stay.

Meanwhile, Queen Victoria took keen interest in the Indian princess, and Gowramma was baptized in her presence in June 1852 at the private chapel in Buckingham Palace. The eleven-year-old princess was named Victoria Gowramma and the Queen became her godmother. She was put under the care of Major Drummond and his wife, who were already familiar with the family while at Benares.

Duleep Singh read about the conversion of Princess Gowramma in the newspapers, and with Dr John Login's subtle suggestions expressed his interest in marrying her as he too was set to embrace the same faith. The English press was quick to compare Princess Victoria Gowramma with Pocahontas, the American Indian princess who embrased Christianity and married a British trader named John Rolfe, and visited London in 1616. Having read a great deal about Britain as well as English literature, Duleep Singh longed to visit England. Dr Login strongly supported this idea and facilitated the trip using his influence with the East India Company. The sixteen-year-old maharaja and his entourage reached London during the midsummer of 1854. Queen Victoria and her consort Prince Albert took an instant liking to the handsome young maharaja and took him under their wings. Queen Victoria and Prince Albert felt accountable for having annexed the young maharaja's

THE PRINCESS GOURAMMA.

The interesting ceremony of the admission into the Christian Church of the Princess Gouramma, daughter of his Highness Prince Vere Rajunder, ex-Rajah of Coorg, was briefly described in the ILLUSTRATED LONDON NEWS of the 3d instant. This, being one of the few instances on record of the abandonment of the Hindoo faith, for the truths of the Christian religion, is an event more than commonly satisfactory to a country whose relations with the great continent of India are so vast and intimate as our own; and we cannot doubt that our readers will be pleased to possess the *vraisemblance* of the interesting Princess and her father, which we are this day enabled to give from a series of portraits recently taken by her Majesty's command.

The ex-Rajah of Coorg is one of those native Princes whose kingdoms have fallen, by their own internal dissensions and weakness, into the power of this country. The ex-Rajah, subsequently to the conquest of his dominions, has been residing at the city of Benares, a sort of state prisoner under the control of the East India Company, but possessing an establishment of ranees (wives) and servants, with an income of about £6000 a year. The Princess Gouramma is the offspring of one of his Highness's favourite ranees, a native of the Coorg country. The Princess was born at Benares, on a Sunday in February, 1841, and her mother died two days afterwards; a circumstance which seems to have led to an increased affection for the child on the part of the ex-Rajah, who, having forfeited his native caste, determined that his favourite daughter should be reared in the principles of the Christian religion, and hence his Highness's visit to England. The ex-Rajah has a family of eleven children, the eldest being a son nineteen years of age. In speaking of them, his Highness shows a marked preference for the Princess Gouramma, whom he describes familiarly as a "pigeon among the crows," "the fairest of the flock," &c. The interest which her Majesty has shown for the Princess, and her Royal condescension in consenting to stand sponsor for the child, cannot fail to have proved highly gratifying to the ex-Rajah. We have already stated that, in addition to her Majesty, the other sponsors were the Viscountess Hardinge, Mrs. Drummond (wife of Major Drummond, 3d Bengal Light Cavalry, who has been appointed by the directors of the East India Company to attend upon his Highness during his absence from India), and Sir James Weir Hogg. The ceremony was performed by the Archbishop of Canterbury, in the private chapel of Buckingham Palace, the Princess receiving from her Majesty the name of "Victoria." When the ex-Rajah, her father, gave up his child into her Majesty's charge, he addressed to her the following instruction and prayer:—
"My dearest daughter—Endeavour to gain every day more and more the grace, and to merit the love and kindness of her most gracious Majesty the Queen; that thereby all Europe, India, and the rest of the world, may hear and be pleased with your good conduct and fame. May heaven bless you, and keep you always under its divine protection and special care! This is my advice to you, my dearest daughter, and my most earnest prayer to the Almighty in your behalf."

The Princess is an interesting and intelligent child. Her complexion is but little darker than that of many Europeans, and her features are regular and pleasing. Her age is only eleven years, but she is far in advance of that period in intelligence. In addition to the Hauree and Hindostanee tongues, she is acquiring English.

The Princess is named after one of the Pagan divinities. A younger sister, the Princess Gungahmah was married, or rather betrothed, to the Nepaulese Prince, Jung Bahadoor, about a year ago, and is now being educated at Nepaul.

By an agreement between the ex-Rajah on the one hand, and the board of directors of the East India Company and the Board of Control on the other, the Princess Gauramma has been placed under her Majesty's protection to be educated in the principles of the Church of England in this country; and her Majesty, having fully considered the matter, has appointed Mrs. Drummond to take charge of the child.

The ex-Rajah will return to Benares in the course of the ensuing autumn.

Article on Princess Gowramma in London Press (1852)

vast territories and having received the famed Kohinoor diamond as a 'gift'.

Queen Victoria was more interested than anyone else in a matrimonial alliance between Duleep Singh and Victoria Gowramma. She wanted to project this couple as 'the bright example' to all Indian royalty. Duleep Singh and Victoria Gowramma met several times at various social events with the British Royal family. The British were happy the way the two blue-blooded Indians got along and hoped the union would soon take place.

By the time Princess Gowramma was fourteen, she had grown to be an intelligent and lively girl. Though not strikingly beautiful, she was attractive. The Indian princess was quite a flirt, making eyes at all the young men including the then

Chikka Veerarajendra and Princess Victoria Gowramma in London (circa 1856)

Princess Victoria Gowramma after her baptism in London

Prince of Wales! Lady Login took her to Rome on a holiday where Duleep Singh and other members of the royal family too were present. Gowramma's coquettish behaviour did not impress the eighteen-year-old Duleep Singh. Duleep Singh later confided in Lady Login that a matrimonial alliance with Gowramma would not work for him. Duleep Singh admitted, 'I am fond of Gowramma, she is wonderful as a friend, but not as a partner for life.'

Duleep Singh was a sensitive young man and was aware that if he were to marry an Indian she would have to convert to Christianity. However, he did not want conversion by anyone just for the opportunity to marry him. He was also not too keen at the time in marrying an European girl, as his children would be half-caste. Prince Albert too tried persuading him to consider marrying Princess Gowramma who was already a Christian. Though it seemed to be an ideal union, Duleep Singh was sure that the alliance would not be good either for him or for Gowramma.

As Gowramma grew, she became increasingly recalcitrant. Her guardians, the Drummonds, found it rather difficult to control the teenager. Though the young princess was disappointed at Duleep Singh having rejected her, she was more interested in a marriage alliance with European nobility. When no marriage proposals were forthcoming, she was depressed and felt lonely. Then one day the Drummonds were shocked to discover Gowramma romantically involved with a stable boy. Soon the whole affair became quite a scandal. At this stage, Queen Victoria intervened and put the girl under the guidance of the Logins.

After the matrimonial alliance with Maharaja Duleep Singh was ruled out, the Logins too found it difficult caring for Gowramma. Lady Login requested the Queen to relieve her as chaperon to the obstinate lass. Gowramma was then placed under the guardianship of Colonel and Lady Catherine Harcourt who lived in Sussex. The young princess was most unhappy with the Harcourts, as they were strict disciplinarians. She was forlorn and miserable, and the rejection by Duleep Singh and absence of marriage proposals continued to demoralize her. With the Western upbringing, she found herself unable to communicate with her father who was fast losing his case against the British in his quest for ownership of the Bombay

Princess Victoria Gowramma in London, 1854

funds. After the Crown took over the administration of India post Sepoy Mutiny in 1857, the ex-raja of Coorg virtually lost all his chances of winning the case. The young princess was depressed with all the gloom surrounding her, and the future looked as bleak as the weather. To add to her unhappiness, her father fell seriously ill. Chikka Veerarajendra died in 1859. His body was temporarily interred in the Kensal Green cemetery. In 1861, the raja's remains were shipped to Benares where his last rites were performed.

Under these disturbing circumstances, Gowramma found comfort in the company of a young butler in the Harcourt

Victoria Gowramma, circa 1860 (Courtesy Mrs Anne Phillips, UK)

household. One night her guardians were horrified to find the young lady trying to elope with the butler, wearing just her petticoat without the stays! This was quite unthinkable in the prudish era of Victorian England. The Harcourts also intercepted amorous letters between the two lovers. Lady Catherine did not wish to continue her responsibilities. It was at this juncture that Maharaja Duleep Singh stepped in to give Princess Gowramma a helping hand as a friend.

Duleep Singh indulged in some matchmaking of his own and introduced the now eighteen-year-old princess to his friend, the dashing Colonel John Campbell, brother of Lady Lena Login. The colonel was thirty years senior to Gowramma and was a man about town. Nevertheless, Cupid struck and after a brief romance, the couple tied the knot in July 1860. A year later, they had a baby girl whom they christened Edith Victoria Gowramma. Within a year of her daughter's birth, Gowramma fell seriously ill with tuberculosis. By then, her marriage to the colonel had soured and she was dejected and unhappy. She suspected that the colonel was more in love with the valuable Coorg jewels inherited by her than in her. She died of consumption in March 1864. This suspicion was further corroborated by the fact that Colonel John Campbell was last seen taking the Coorg crown jewels of his deceased wife to be deposited in Coutts Bank in London. Neither he nor the precious jewels were ever seen again. Queen Victoria was profoundly saddened by the demise of the young princess. In her epitaph engraved on Gowramma's grave in Brompton cemetery, the queen quoted St John:

'... other sheep I have, which are not of this fold.'

Victoria Gowramma's daughter, Edith Victoria, married Capt. Henry Edward Yardley in 1882. Their only son, Henry Victor Yarley, emigrated to Australia in 1914. His decendants live in New South Wales.

(A more detailed account of Victoria Gowramma's story can be read in the book *Victoria Gowramma: The Lost Princess of Coorg*, by C.P. Belliappa, published by Rupa Publications.)

FREEDOM MOVEMENT IN COORG

The overthrow of the last raja of Coorg in 1834 and the subsequent British administration brought a great deal of progress in Coorg. As described in earlier chapters, education, development of infrastructure, introduction of coffee and above all an equitable law brought peace and prosperity to the land. For nearly seventy-five years, the British ruled the province without any resistance from the local populace.

However, by early twentieth-century, there was growing disillusionment with colonial rule. People in Coorg too yearned for freedom as this movement was gaining ground in other parts of India.

It was in the year 1909 that an organization named 'Jamindars' Society' was started by Rao Bahadur Codanda Madaiah and Biddanda Ganapathy, to recommend to the British government on issues relevant to the people of Kodagu. In 1912, this Society was reorganized as Jamindars' Sangha. Membership of this Sangha swelled and its presence was felt in every village in Kodagu. Jamindars' Sangha became a powerful voice of the people.

In 1921, a need was felt to start a newspaper in Kodagu. Most of the prominent members of Jamindars' Sangha joined hands to start the *Kodagu* newspaper. With Pandiyanda I. Belliappa as the first editor, this publication soon became very popular and gave substantial boost in increasing awareness in people towards their rights.

Jamindars' Sangha laid the foundation for the establishment of National Congress Party in Kodagu. About thirty-five members from Kodagu participated in the Congress Session presided over by Mahatma Gandhi at Belgaum in 1924. Inspired by this meeting, it was decided to start a chapter of Congress Party in Kodagu. On 4 January 1925, Kodagu Zilla Congress Committee was formed with Paruvangada Kushalappa as the president. C.N. Venkappaiah was named the honorary secretary and M.M. Siddique as the treasurer. The party started with fifteen members. In February 1925, a Khadi Bhandar was opened in Virajpet. People enthusiastically took up spinning cotton with charakas supplied by the Congress Party. The trio of the Jamindars' Sangha, the *Kodagu* newspaper and the Congress Party, took the message of self-rule to every corner in Kodagu.

On 26 January 1930 'Purna Swaraj' was declared by the leaders of the freedom struggle. People in Kodagu wholeheartedly took part in this movement. For the first time, a public meeting was organized in Gonicoppal, to spread the call for Swaraj given by Mahatma Gandhiji. At this public meeting, C.N. Venkappaiah, Manepanda Chinnappa, Kollimada Carumbaiah and Machimanda Muthanna spoke. Many senior leaders from Karnataka Congress such as Allur Venkata Rao, Ranganath Diwakar and Kamaladevi Chattopadaya et al., started visiting Kodagu to train and motivate local leaders. Besides, litterateurs Da Ra Bendre, K.V. Puttappa, Masti Venkatesh Iyengar and D.V. Gundappa also made frequent trips to Kodagu to enthuse the people in fighting for freedom.

In Ponnampet, a large open area was named Kushalpura in memory of Paruvangada Kushalappa who suddenly died in

1928, at the age of thirty-eight, while on his way back from Calcutta where he was one of the delegates from Kodagu at the Congress session. Every last Sunday of the month, Indian national flag was hoisted at Kushalpura. Ajjikuttira Chinnappa and Mallegada Chengappa were the first to hoist the national flag at this venue on 26 May 1929. The Swadeshi movement received wide support from the citizens. People started shunning imported goods, and wearing Khadi became popular. The dangers of alcohol consumption were made aware to the public. Many protested against sale of alcohol in Kodagu. Bajjans, Harikathas, and dramas were organized in villages to spread Indian culture and heritage. Well-known exponent of Harikatha, Belur Keshavdas, visited Kodagu, and his rendering of stories from the epics enthralled the people and induced patriotism. The local British government was rattled by these activities. For the first time, section 144 was imposed in Kodagu, and Keshavdas was prevented from holding his Harikathas. Mahatma Gandhiji's 'Dandi March' and 'Salt Satyagraha' were actively supported by the people of Kodagu. The struggle for freedom took deeper roots.

In 1930, under the leadership of Pandiyanda I. Belliappa, the government was given an ultimatum to close liquor shops in Kodagu. When this was not heeded, on 10 June 1930 large number of activists picketed peacefully in front of liquor shops at Ponnampet. Soon similar picketing started in other towns and villages. Liquor sales dropped affecting revenue for the government.

Around this time, women in Kodagu decided to enter the freedom struggle and support their male counterparts. Kotera Accavva was the first woman to take this plunge. Many women followed. Picketing against liquor consumption became highly effective with women taking part in the movement. On 30 May 1930 an impressive rally by the womenfolk was held in Madikeri which included two of the well-known Poovaiah sisters—Chitra and Latha. The talented sisters gave up their education and became satyagrahis. It was during this time that a young eighteen-year-old Kavery, daughter of Kolera Cariappa, asked permission from her father to take part in the proposed picketing at Hudikeri on 15 September 1930. She was heart-broken when her father refused. Kavery, filled with intense patriotism, could not bear the disappointment. The following day Kavery took the extreme step of taking her own life by jumping in the lake nearby. Kavery's actions kindled the desire for freedom amongst scores of youth in Kodagu.

Protest rallies against liquor sales and rejection of imported goods intensified. On 20 September 1930, satyagrahis were arrested for the first time in Kodagu. Those who courted arrest included Pandiyanda Belliappa, Kollimada Carumbaiah, H.R. Krishnaiah and Abdul Gaffoor Khan. In addition, the newspaper *'Kodagu'* was brought under press ordinance, because of which publication had to be stopped till a caution deposit of 1,000 rupees was paid to the government. All these measures spurred the citizens to protest against British rule with added vigour.

Some of young satyagrahis took more proactive steps to register their determination to end foreign rule. On 17 December 1930, three brave young men: Mallegada Chengappa, B.G. Ganapaiah and Mandepanda Cariappa entered Madikeri Fort and boldly removed the Union Jack and in its place hoisted the Indian national flag. They happily courted arrest for their patriotic act.

The British government started arresting and imprisoning satyagrahis in the hope that they could curb the freedom movement. To their dismay, the movement gained further support. More and more young men and women joined the struggle in response to the call by Mahatma Gandhi. Amongst those who discontinued their studies and joined the freedom movement was my father, then twenty-year-old Chepudira M. Poonacha from Gonicoppal.

On 7 January 1932, the government imposed section 144 all over Kodagu, and holding of any rallies was banned for a month. Defying this ban, on 10 January 1932, a huge public meeting was held at Gonicoppal. Pandiyand Belliappa and Ajjikuttira Chinnappa addressed the satyagrahis. Many leaders were arrested and had to serve sentences ranging from six to nine months in Kannur prison. On 27 January 1932, women satyagrahis Pandiyanda Seetha Belliappa, Baliyatanda Muddavva and Mukkatira Bojamma were arrested for distributing pamphlets to the public.

Around this time, Chepudira Poonacha was given the task of composing, cyclostyling and distribution of a publication named *Veerabharati*. He did this successfully from his estate near Gonicoppal, and the authorities were unable to locate the origin of the publication. Extensive searches were made to trace the cyclostyling machine. When the machine was finally discovered, Chepudira Poonacha was sentenced to nine months rigorous imprisonment at Kannur jail. This was his second of the three stints in prison. He, however, had the good fortune of coming in contact with many national leaders while in prison. Amongst them were C. Rajagopalchari, Prof. N.G. Ranga, Acharya Kripalani et al., who took classes for the young freedom fighters.

In 1934, Pandiyanda Belliappa, Kollimada Carumbaiah, Chepudira Poonacha and other leaders requested Mahatma Gandhiji to visit Kodagu. Gandhiji toured Kodagu from 21 to 23 February, and was impressed by the intensity of freedom struggle in this picturesque hilly region. He urged the local people to do more for the upliftment of downtrodden whom he called Harijans (God's people).

During a public meeting, Gandhiji said, 'Since my arrival here I am enjoying the beauty of nature. I deem it that just as your country's nature is beautiful, your hearts also must be beautiful. I understand there is no temple entry for untouchables. But, if the Harijans are not allowed into temples, I do not say that your hearts are beautiful. Learn from nature and wash off the impurities from your heart.'

This statement had a profound impact on the people of Coorg. Soon a 'Harijan Fund' was established, and many women voluntarily came forward and donated money and their jewellery to the Mahatma. More people started wearing Khadi and observed the Swadeshi philosophy. Age-old discriminations against Harijans started to wane. Harijans and Girijans too began to take part in the freedom movement, and many of them courted arrest and prison terms.

With the Second World War breaking out in 1939, there was a lull in the Satyagraha movement all over the nation. Gandhiji, however, continued the call for independence on the foundation of non-violence. His 'ahimsa' philosophy was spontaneously accepted by the satyagrahis in Kodagu. Satyagraha Samithis were founded all over Kodagu. On 11 May 1940 the first Satyagraha training centre was started in Virajpet. Pandiyanda

Belliappa, his wife Seetha, Kollimada Carumbaiah, Mallengada Chengappa, Kakamada Nanaiah, Chepudira M. Poonacha and many other leaders took the pledge to continue Satyagraha peacefully, and practice ahimsa.

On 8 August 1942, Mahatma Gandhiji made his momentous call 'Quit India' at the All India Congress Committee meeting held at Bombay. This had an electrifying effect on the entire nation. Many leaders were arrested. Chepudira M. Poonacha, who was present at this meeting, was arrested on 14 August 1942.

The long struggle for gaining freedom was finally realized on 15 August 1947. Houses were decorated all over Kodagu, and lamps were lit to usher in freedom at midnight. Students took processions in Madikeri and other towns. Pandiyanda Belliappa and Kollimada Carumbaiah addressed the celebrating crowds. Chepudira M. Poonacha was in the Central Hall of the Parliament in Delhi where Jawaharlal Nehru made his historic midnight speech. Also present at the venue was the then Brigadier K.M. Cariappa, who was later appointed as the first Indian commander-in-chief of the armed forces. Post independence, Chepudira M. Poonacha occupied important positions such as: member of the constituent assembly, chief minister of Coorg State, home minister of Karnataka, union railway minister and governor of Madhya Pradesh and Orissa.

A community hall has been constructed in Gonicoppal in honour of all those from Kodagu who made sacrifices in securing freedom that we enjoy today.

GENESIS OF MERGER OF COORG WITH KARNATAKA

1834 was a watershed year in the history of Coorg. So was 1956, when it ceased to be a Part 'C' state and was merged with Karnataka. Dewan Chepudira Ponnappa was one of the central figures during the overthrow of the last king of the Haleri dynasty. In a strange twist of fate, his great-great-grandson Chepudira M. Poonacha was a pivotal personality during the merger of Coorg with Karnataka.

The leaders involved in the freedom movement envisaged the concept of demarcating India on linguistic basis as far back as the early 1920s. The idea of Coorg becoming a part of the Vishal Mysore State which was to include the Kannada speaking areas from Bombay–Karnataka, Hyderabad–Karnataka, Madras Presidency and Old Mysore was placed before the Belgaum Congress presided over by Mahatma Gandhiji in 1924. This movement gained momentum when the Coorg Congress Party was brought under the Karnataka Pradesh Congress Committee in the 1930s with its headquarters at Dharwad. A legislative council of twenty members was established in Coorg in accordance with the Federal Act passed in 1935.

At the time of independence in 1947, India had around 600 states. Most of these were princely states of varying sizes. There were the large states directly ruled by the British known as British Provinces or Presidencies. These included Bombay,

Madras, Punjab, Central Provinces, United Provinces, Bengal and Bihar. Then there were a few smaller states directly under the British, administered by a chief commissioner. These were: Bhopal, Bilaspur, Kutch, Ajmeer-Merwara, Himachal Pradesh, Vindya Pradesh, Manipur, Tripura, Delhi and Coorg.

The Constitution of India was brought into force on 26 January 1950. The earlier British Provinces were categorized as Part 'A' states; the princely states were Part 'B' states, and the regions administered by chief commissioners were known as Part 'C' states.

Though the British ruled as an imperial power, independent India had to be administered as a democracy. The leadership had to device a system for the effective administration of the newly formed nation. In order to achieve this objective, it was imperative that the states would have to be reorganized into more manageable sizes. The rationale for states reorganization was already decided to be on the basis of language. In a vast, diverse and complex country like India, language was the only common denominator that could be thought of to keep groups of varied populations together. This idea found acceptance amongst a majority of people in this new nation.

A 'States Reorganization Committee' was set-up to go into the entire process of deciding on the areas which should be part of a state depending on the language spoken. Based on the recommendations of this Committee, a 'States Reorganization Commission' was formed under Justice Fazal Ali with a mandate from the parliament. At this point in time, Chepudira M. Poonacha was a member of the Constituent Assembly (and the only Kodava signatory to the Constitution of India). He deposed before the Commission, and initially argued in favour of retaining Coorg as a state. Likewise, there were oppositions to reorganization from several other areas in the country that had enjoyed statehood under the British.

In 1952, the country had its first general elections. The question of merger became an important election issue in Coorg. Some of the stalwarts in Coorg politics led by Pandiyanda I. Belliappa vehemently opposed the merger of Coorg. They subsequently broke away from Congress and formed a separate group known as the 'Coorg Separatist Party'. Out of the twenty-four seats in the Coorg Legislative Assembly, seven seats went to this new party. In 1952, C.M. Poonacha was elected as the chief minister and K. Mallappa as the home minister; B.S. Kushalappa was chosen as the speaker of the House. Colonel Daya Singh Bedi, was appointed as the chief commissioner by the central government. Coorg was one of the well-administered states, and was hailed as a model Part 'C' state in the country.

There were a number of meetings of the chief ministers of all Part 'C' states. Senior leaders like Jawaharlal Nehru, Sardar Patel, Govind Vallabh Pant, Lal Bhadur Shastri et al., prevailed on princely states and the chief ministers of Part 'C' states to accept the recommendations of the States Reorganization Commission (SRC) in the larger interest of the nation. Besides, there seemed no compelling reasons for these small states (with the exception of Himachal Pradesh) to remain as they did under the British rule. Tripura and Manipur were made Union Territories, and got statehood in 1972. Being the capital of the nation, an exception was made in the case of Delhi as well.

The Coorg government finally agreed with the SRC and it was thus decided by the ruling Congress Party to merge the state with the then Vishal Mysore State. This issue was debated at length in the Coorg Legislative Assembly on 6 December 1955. The motion was put to vote. Twenty-two out of the twenty-four members voted in favour of merger. Surprisingly, five out of the seven members of the Coorg Separatist Party including Pandiyanda Belliappa voted in favour of merger! K.P. Karumbaiah and P.C. Uthaiah cast the two dissenting votes. However, 'consent' by the Part 'A', Part 'B' and Part 'C' states, was merely a formality. The decision to reorganize the Indian states as per the recommendations of SRC was a foregone conclusion taken by the highest law making authority—the Indian Parliament.

Despite opposition in various other parts of the proposed Kannada speaking state (renamed Karnataka in 1973), the Vishal Mysore State formally came in being on 1 November 1956. S. Nijalingappa was sworn in as the first chief minister of the new state. C.M. Poonacha from Coorg was taken into the cabinet as minister for home and industries. B.S. Kushalappa was the pro-tem speaker of the state assembly.

There has been a growing sense of anguish over the years on the issue of the circumstances that reduced Coorg from being a self-governed state to a minor district in Karnataka. However, whatever may be the arguments on merger, the states' reorganization on linguistic basis could not have been forestalled. The whole process was ratified under an Act of Parliament brought about by the 7th Amendment to the Constitution of India. This rearrangement, which affected many parts of the country, was in the larger interest of the newly independent nation.

Whether Coorg has benefited after the merger with

Karnataka is debatable. Hypothetically, had Coorg remained a separate state there is no doubt it would have been one of the most prosperous areas in the country. In spite of verbal assurances given to the people of Coorg regarding preserving the land and its culture, several of these promises have been broken. Forest wealth and environment have suffered heavily after the merger. The level of corruption got integrated with that of the rest of the state. The main grouse of a majority of the people is the lack of developmental work in the district. Being the smallest district in the state, Coorg lacks political clout. The leadership in Bangalore goes on the premise that the district has the best per capita income in the state, and therefore could be pushed to the bottom of the list of priorities. This attitude has spawned a movement demanding restoration of statehood for Coorg that is Kodagu.

On the positive side, employment opportunities saw an upswing for the people of Coorg in the earlier years after merger. Large scale recruiting was done in departments such as police, forest, state administration and public sector undertakings. Educational opportunities too increased for those seeking collegiate and professional qualifications.

Kodavas as a community have to an extent lost their cultural identity with Kodagu. The Coorgs enjoyed the status of a dominant minority since the time of the nayakas, the Haleri rajas and the British. However, democratic India has taken away the privileged position enjoyed by the community for centuries. This was bound to happen in a democratic system. On account of hundred per cent literacy and the relatively well-spread economic status, the Kodavas are categorized as a forward class. With the passage of time, a significant number of Kodavas have prospered in various fields having migrated to other parts of Karnataka, India and outside the country as well.

GLOSSARY

Ahimsa	Non-violence
Aramane	Palace
Ainmane	Family house of a patriarchal clan
Brahma-Rakshasa	Demon
Chikka	Junior
Desadrohi	Traitor
Dewan	Highest army and civilian position
Dodda	Elder
Dulli-batha	Dusty remnants after cleaning freshly harvested paddy
Devarakadu	Sacred grove
Edde-bojana	Leftover meal from the royal kitchen
Gullige kala	Auspicious time of the day
Guru-karana	Ancestors
Ghat	Mountain range
Harijan	God's people (the downtrodden)
Harikatha	Folklore
Jagir	Land-lordship
Jangama	Priest
Kachampuli	A souring agent from fermented wild fruit essential in some of the Coorg dishes
Kadanga	Trenches to demarcate territories. Also for defence
Kailpodu	Kodava festival celebrated in September

Kaimada	A commemorative mantap
Kariakara	Army commander
Khadi	Cloth made from home-spun cotton
Sarva Kariakara	Senior army commander
Karnanika	Accountant
Kombu	Horn-shaped brass trumpet
Kunta	Lame
Kupiya and Chele	Traditional attire of Coorg (Kodava) men, comprising of a long black overlapping coat (kupiya), bound at the waist by an embroidered red sash (chele)
Machaan	Platform built on treetops during hunts
Mahaswami	Respectful term used while addressing the rajas
Makka-parije	A practice amongst the Kodavas in the absence of a male heir, to facilitate the inheritance of landed property
Mantra	Religious chants
Mutt	Hindu religious missionary
Mantap	Structure for performing weddings. Also built to commemorate a deity or hero
Nari-mangala	Special event akin to a wedding ceremony when a tiger is heroically slain
Nayaka	King or a chieftain
Odikathi	A short broad-bladed combat knife
Okka	Patrilineal family unit
Ooru-thakka	Headman of a village
Seme-thakka	Headman of a group of villages
Desa-thakka	Headman of a province
Palegars	A minor chieftain

Puttari	Harvest festival
Rahu kala	Inauspicious time of the day
Sarva Kariakara	Senior army commander
Satyagraha	Civil disobedience
Satyagrahis	Freedom fighters
Shanti pooja	Ritual to appease the departed souls
Shikar	Hunt
Shiva-linga	Stone phallus symbol used in worship
Siddis	African origin bodyguards and executioners
Siribai	Hare-lipped (a deformity of the upper lip)
Swaraj	Freedom
Tantric	Practitioner of the occult
Thombarada-oota	Food served to the common man at the palace
Toddy	A local brew made out of palm sap
Topiwalas	Derogatory term for the French
Vamsha	Family
Veera-boomi	Land of the braves
Zenana	Harem

REFERENCES

Gazetteer of Coorg, Rev. G. Richter, 1870
Coorg Memoirs: An Account of Coorg, Rev. H. Moegling, 1855
Kodagina Itihasa, D.N. Krishnayya, 1974 (in Kannada)
Gazetteer of Mysore and Coorg, Benjamin Lewis Rice, 1878
Queen Victoria's Maharaja—Duleep Singh, Michael Alexander & Sushila Anand, Phoenix Press, 1980
The Men Who Ruled India, Philip Mason, Rupa & Co., 1985
Gazetteer of India, Karnataka, Kodagu District, 1993
100 Elite Clubs of India, Bhageria Foundation, New Delhi, 2006

ACKNOWLEDGEMENTS

The idea of compiling a book on the history of Coorg (Kodagu) for story form occurred to me after I started writing a column for P.T. Bopanna's website: www.coorgtourisminfo.com

I would like to thank Bopanna for giving me a platform, and for kindling my interest which made me delve in detail into the past of Coorg. Some of the episodes have appeared in the website in a much shorter form.

I would like to thank my sister and reputed writer Kavery and her husband Vijay Nambisan for their valuable suggestions and advice.

My thanks to members of Thathanda, Kongettira, Ajjikuttira and Chepudira families for sharing their knowledge of Coorg history, and giving me access to some old paintings and artefacts.

This book would not have been possible without the encouragement of the publisher, Mr Kapish Mehra of Rupa & Co. I thank him profusely. I would also like to thank Milee Ashwarya for her painstaking efforts in editing this book.

Finally, I would like to thank my wife Aruna, son Vikram, and daughter-in-law Dechu for their unflinching support.

C.P. Belliappa
Coorg